Just a Cowboy's Dream Come True

Flyboys of Sweet Briar Ranch in North Dakota
Book Twelve
Jessie Gussman

Published By: Jessie Gussman

Contents

Acknowledgements

Cover art by Julia Gussman
Editing by Heather Hayden
Narration by Jay Dyess
Author Services by CE Author Assistant

Listen to a FREE professionally performed and produced audiobook version of this title on Youtube. Search for "Say With Jay" to browse all available FREE Dyess/Gussman audiobooks.

Chapter 1

Carna Long put her car in park and stared at the farmhouse and grounds.

Sweet Briar Ranch.

A new start. A new life.

Beside her on the passenger seat, Posey whined and stretched, lifting her head and pointing her nose in the air as though better able to catch the scents that drifted in through the partially open window.

"Hang on a second, Posey," Carna murmured, needing a moment to compose herself.

Her brother, Smith, had told her there would be a job for Posey and her here and a place to stay.

Everything she owned was in the car she drove, which had miraculously held together on the long trip from New Hampshire.

She'd tried as hard as she could to save her grandparents' farm, but in the end, the only thing she'd saved had been Posey.

She hadn't quite gotten over that bitter disappointment and had a hard time mustering any enthusiasm to be in North Dakota, although she appreciated the fact that she had a job and family. Her brother. Even if she didn't know him that well since it had been years since they'd spent any amount of time together. Not only because of Smith's time in the Air Force, but because Carna had been busy working day and night trying to keep their grandparents' farm from going bankrupt.

Her eyes swept the area in front of her again. She'd texted Smith just a bit ago and let him know she was coming, but she didn't see him, or anyone, around. Then she blinked and did a double take.

There was a Highland steer standing beside the chicken coop.

She'd seen pictures of Highlands, and was vaguely familiar with them, but had never been close to one. Still, it was unmistakable with the shaggy fur and the long horns.

Horns that, unless she was mistaken, had just gotten caught in the latch of the chicken coop, and...as he shook his head, the latch jiggled open and the door swung wide.

The steer moseyed away, like he hadn't noticed that he had just opened the coop door, but the chickens had no such compunctions.

As a unit, they flew and ran for the door, like some sort of signal had gone through the entire fenced chicken yard, one that sent them all running for freedom.

Posey whined as Carna grabbed her door handle to get out.

"All right. You can come." Posey was used to working on the farm. Maybe it was Carna's imagination, but she seemed to get more depressed the further away they got from New Hampshire, like she knew she was never going to see her home again.

Knowing the chickens were soon going to be too scattered to even attempt to round up, Carna hopped out of the car, holding the door for Posey to jump out, then slammed it and jogged over to the melee.

But she was too late. It would be impossible to catch the chickens now. They would have to wait until evening when they roosted. Chickens were always easier to catch at night. They had a tendency to not move around much at all once darkness fell. Of course, finding them wherever they roosted would be the challenge.

Just then, barking made her jerk her head to the right as a dog, low to the ground, ears back, raced toward them, startling and chasing first one chicken and then another.

"Hey!" Carna said, going forward, even though she knew it was dangerous to attempt to grab a strange dog. But still, she couldn't just stand there while it attacked the chickens and possibly killed them.

"Pepper. Down!" a deep male voice called, and the dog stopped immediately, falling to the ground in a crouch, his ears back, his head rolling to the side as he looked for the man who had called to him.

The man, clad in jeans and a T-shirt with worn low-heeled, square-toed work boots and a cowboy hat pulled low over his eyes, walked toward her.

Because of the hat, she couldn't see the expression on his face other than his flat lips, which sliced a thin line over his square and jutting jaw.

A muscle twitched there.

He was angry, and Carna had to fight back the shot of anxiety that zipped through her. She hadn't done anything wrong. She tried to calm herself by saying that she didn't have to worry about his anger, because it was not going to be directed at her.

"Ma'am. You need to get back in your car and go to the guest entrance. This is our private quarters. And you don't ever open an animal pen without permission. Whether here or at anyone else's ranch." The man didn't exactly snarl at her, but it was obvious he was holding onto his patience by a fraying thread.

Carna opened her mouth and then closed it again. He thought she was a guest?

She wore jeans and boots and a T-shirt, similar to his outfit, although several sizes smaller most definitely, and she didn't have the cowboy hat. Back east, her boots were pushing the limits of what people thought was ridiculous; the cowboy hat would practically land her in queue for the insane asylum.

Still, she had to defend herself. The man was mistaken.

"I didn't open the chicken door. The steer did it."

The man stumbled, then caught himself immediately. He snorted and then lifted his hat, running a hand through his hair as though he needed a moment to compose himself so that he could speak lucidly.

"Of course. The steer opened the chicken pen." He shook his head. "Now I've heard it all. Lady, get back into your car, go back to where the road forks, and take the other lane. That will take you to the guest quarters. They can deal with you there."

"I sure hope you're not dealing with guests. As rude as you are," Carna mumbled, unable to keep her opinion to herself when she knew she should.

Still, the man was odious and arrogant. The idea that she would lie. Of course, the idea that the steer opened the chicken pen was probably just as laughable to him as it was to her.

"I'm not a guest," she managed to say to the man as he took two steps away from her, like their conversation was finished.

"Then you're a trespasser," the man said flatly. It wasn't a question.

"I belong here. I'm Smith's sister, Carna. And you are?" She held out her hand and tried to keep the superior note out of her voice. Smith might not be the sole owner of the place, but she knew for a fact that the Sweet Briar Ranch had been started by Smith's crew, and Smith was the commander. Regardless of whether they were out of the Air Force or not, he would be given an extra dose of respect, if she didn't miss her guess.

The man froze, then he turned toward her slowly, his eyes narrowed, his head slightly tilted as though he were trying to see something in her that he expected to be able to pick out.

The look made her uncomfortable, like she was hiding something.

Not to mention, she felt stupid with her hand out while the man made no move to touch it.

She was about to take it away when a slow grin tilted up the corners of the man's mouth.

He was handsome wearing a frown; he was devastating with that slow grin that made the little dimple at the corner of his mouth pop.

It was a familiar dimple, and she had the sudden urge to turn on her toes and march right back to her car, drive past the fork in the road, and go somewhere, anywhere, else.

"Carna? Smith's bratty little sister? Man, kid. I wouldn't have recognized your looks, but I suppose you're still just as big of an annoyance now as you used to be."

Maybe he didn't mean to be so insulting; he did seem a little flabbergasted and slightly shocked.

She'd told Smith she wasn't quite sure what day she would arrive since she had to stay at the farm in New Hampshire for an indefinite amount of time, until the new owners had gotten their sea legs.

They were from the city and had never run a farm before.

It had been bittersweet, teaching them to do all the things she knew by heart. Showing them the quirks and foibles of the farm that she loved.

Maybe Smith hadn't told anyone she was coming since her arrival had been so up in the air.

The dimple winked at her, and a memory flashed. It couldn't be.

"Miller?" Smith's best friend from high school, their neighbor, and her nemesis.

His smug look confirmed her guess.

"And you're just as arrogant and conceited as you always were." She grunted. "And just as likely to jump to the absolute wrong conclusion as well."

"You told me the steer opened the chicken coop. Tater Tot, come on." Miller lifted his hands, then slapped them down against his pants. He looked around and then indicated the birds that flapped through the yard. As Carna looked across the wide expanse of grass, two of them hopped up on the porch.

It was cute, but wherever chickens were, they left their markings behind, and nobody wanted that on their porch. Particularly a dude ranch that was trying to impress people from the city, who would never understand that in order to have cute chickens, you had to have the cute chicken coop to go along with it.

"I didn't lie. I never have. I sat in my car and watched that steer use his horn to open the chicken coop. Now whether he did it on purpose or not—"

"I'm sure he did," Miller said, in a condescending tone that made her feel like she was five again. She wanted to stamp her foot. He'd always gotten under her skin. Found a way to tease her and make her so mad she wanted to spit.

Apparently, the dozen or so years since she'd last seen him hadn't changed anything for either one of them.

"Fine. I know it sounds crazy, but it's the truth."

"I'm sure it is, Tater Tot," he said, again using the nickname she'd hated as a child. No one but Miller ever used it, and she'd totally forgot about it.

"Whatever, Ducky Doo Doo," she said derisively, that name she used to call him in return coming easily to her lips. She was ashamed at how easily it came.

His lips twitched in what she almost thought could have been a genuine smile, but he clamped it down immediately.

"Tell me you're just passing through," he said, his hands on his hips, looking at the chickens that happily picked their way through the yard.

"I can tell you that, but it wouldn't be true. And one of us doesn't like to lie, Ducky," she tacked that name on at the end again, just for spite. Or maybe because she wanted to see if she could make him smile again.

No, that couldn't be it at all.

"You're kidding, right? You're just trying to ruin my day."

"You don't have to believe me. But it's the truth."

He took a deep breath, pulling it in through his nose and looking up at the sky like he was pleading with the Almighty for patience.

When he looked back down, his face still seemed tight, like he was not as re-laxed as he wanted her to think he was.

"Welcome to Sweet Briar, Tater. You go on up to the house. Darby will be there, and she'll take care of you. Do me a favor, and remind her that I'm working with the more seasoned guests, and I'd like to be stationed as far away from you as possible. Which, I'm sure, suits you as well." His jaw jutted out, and his lips pursed.

"Of course it does, Ducky. I'll be sure to ask Darby to have me working as far away from you as possible. After all, there's a reason you have Doo Doo in your nickname."

"That happened one time," he said immediately.

"For you. Zero for me. That's one area where I'll admit you have me beat."

She allowed an evil little smile to turn up her lips. She really didn't want to fight with Miller. He seemed like he'd turned into a halfway decent guy. But he hadn't been nice to her, and he was treating her like she hadn't grown up at all.

Surely it was obvious that she had. She'd single-handedly been taking care of her grandparents' farm for the last three years. If there had been a way to save it, she would have found it. She didn't need to be treated like a child who had never set foot on a farm before. And the idea that she would go over and let chickens out on purpose was just ludicrous.

Obviously, Miller hadn't changed at all.

So he deserved to be teased for something that he'd done as a child, since he'd been treating her like a two-year-old since she set foot on the place.

"When you grow up and are able to let it go, let me know, Tater." He started to walk and called over his shoulder, "Pepper, heel." Pepper immediately jumped up, ran to Miller's side, and obediently followed him as he walked away.

Carna let her eyes linger on the broad shoulders for just a moment before she turned away. She didn't need to watch that.

Also, she was a little irrationally irritated at the dog for being so...obedient.

She should have checked with Smith a little more thoroughly about what was going on here before she jumped on the chance to come out. She'd just been happy to have a place to live. She'd sunk every last penny she had into trying to save her grandparents' farm, and she really had no other place to go. This had seemed like a lifesaver at the time, but if she was going to have to be face-to-face with Miller every day, maybe it wasn't going to be as good as what she thought.

Shooting a few quick texts off to Smith – she wouldn't want Miller to get to him first and give him the wrong version of what happened – Carna had a small back-and-forth with him before she shoved her phone back in her pocket. There. Miller could say what he wanted. Smith knew the truth.

Calling Posey, who had been sitting and staring at her the whole time, she walked toward the house.

Posey, shoving her wet nose into Carna's hand, whined, like she was asking Carna to give Miller the benefit of the doubt just to get along.

"No. He's a jerk, and I absolutely do not want to have anything to do with him."

Chapter 2

"So I heard you got acquainted with Carna earlier today," Smith said as he walked into the barn where Miller was mucking out a horse stall.

Miller leaned his fork up and looked at Smith. "You could have warned me."

"Why? I heard you had quite a meeting."

"Because I would have recognized her. Maybe. She's grown up some since I last saw her, but at least I would have been ready, because you know she always rubs me the wrong way."

"But you haven't seen her for years. I thought you would have grown out of whatever childhood animosity was between the two of you."

"She's just a diva the way she always was," Miller said, picking his fork back up and shoving it in the shavings. He didn't really mean it. She'd turned into a beautiful young woman, with long flowing hair and a ready smile. She still had a dog at her heels, which hadn't changed, and she'd been just as sassy as she'd always been.

He had certainly been more than a little surprised to find out that the woman he thought was lost and purposely letting the chickens out was Carna. That probably set him on the defensive, as much as seeing the chickens running around the yard and hearing her say she hadn't opened the pen.

"She let the chickens out. Did she tell you that?"

"No. She told me Billy did it."

"That was the story she tried to give me too. You're not buying it, are you?" It was ridiculous. The idea that the steer would have opened the pen was totally unbelievable.

"I've never known Carna to lie. I mean, she was an annoying little sister, but she wasn't dishonest. You can give her that much."

Smith had come over and leaned his shoulder against the post at the corner of the stall. He put a hand up to stroke the muzzle of Walker, the horse who was on stall rest because of the abscess in his front left foot.

Miller wanted to say an automatic no, but Smith was right. Carna had been annoying but not dishonest. Still, it grated for him to give her any kind of benefit of the doubt. They always seemed to have some kind of competition going on between the two of them, and to give her any slack was to give her a leg up, and he just couldn't let her "win."

"Maybe. I don't really remember her lying, but that doesn't mean she didn't," Miller finally muttered.

Smith belted out a laugh. "You know, it wouldn't have surprised me if you two would have ended up together. In fact, you might have if she and I hadn't moved."

"No. That was never going to happen. And it still isn't, so don't get any ideas. I'm quite happy here, alone."

"No one's really happy alone," Smith said, sounding reasonable. But Miller stopped him.

"Spoken like a married man. But I don't have to share my bed, I don't have to cook if I don't feel like it, I don't have anybody nagging me that I'm not putting stuff in the right spot, I can be grumpy and miserable, and I can go to bed without a shower anytime I want."

"Right. You're just basically arguing in favor of you needing a wife, because the rest of us have to live with you like that."

Smith's words were easy, and he had a friendly grin on his face.

"Whatever. I've never heard you complain."

"That's just because we don't want to hurt your feelings."

"That's new," Miller muttered as Smith huffed out a laugh.

Then his expression sobered. "Carna is out in the kitchen, helping Darby make lunch for tomorrow. I've hired her, and you're going to have to learn to get along with her."

"I told her wherever she was working, I would do something on the opposite end of the ranch. That way, we won't have any trouble getting along."

Smith looked at the post where his hand rested, as though thinking about what he was about to say. He started slowly. "Well, you know, we've stretched our finances to the limit, and we need to bring in a pile of tours this summer."

Miller sobered up immediately. He didn't do the books, but everybody who worked on the farm had access to the finances. They believed that if everyone had an idea of what was going on, everyone would be able to make suggestions on how to improve things.

"I know. Marketing isn't exactly my thing, but if there's something I can do—"

"Actually, funny you should mention that. I hired Carna with the idea that she would do the three-day dude ranch competition that's going to be held outside of Billings, Montana, next week."

"So I don't have to go anymore?" Miller said, surprised, since Smith had just been saying that everyone needed to pull their share. He had been planning on going and had some hopes that he would actually do well in some of the competitions.

"No. You're still going, and so is she. I thought the two of you would make a cute couple, and the ranch would be better served if it could be billed as a romantic destination spot."

"Wait." Miller stopped, jabbing his manure fork into a pile of shavings and holding it with one hand while he wrapped his other hand around his neck. "Did you just say that I'm supposed to pretend to be a couple with your sister?"

"I didn't exactly say that, but that would be ideal."

"Isn't there supposed to be some kind of man code where you can't date your best friend's little sister?"

"Is there? I've never heard of that?"

Miller was pretty sure he'd heard that somewhere, but he couldn't really place where. He supposed it didn't matter, since he had no interest in Carna either way.

"I'm not saying you have to be interested in her, and I'm not saying it has to be real. I'm just saying that it might benefit the ranch if you pretended. But if you can't stand each other, then don't. But I'm still signing you two up for the couple's competition, rather than the individual ones. I think it will be better advertising."

Miller didn't say anything but finished getting the last of the wet sawdust shavings out of the stall before going over and grabbing a bale of fresh shavings to put in on top of the bedding.

"I told you I would do whatever you needed me to. I can't guarantee that Carna's going to cooperate, but you know I will."

He probably shouldn't have made that dig on Carna. He really didn't know her anymore. But he remembered her as more of a diva who wanted her own way than someone who was a team player.

Miller used his knife to slice the bag open before he spread shavings around the stall. He wanted to insist to Smith that he would work as far away from Carna as he could, but even more than that, he wanted to be a help to the ranch. He had been one of the ones who wanted to expand as quickly as they could, knowing that they were going to tax their resources and their finances.

It was a gamble he had been willing to take, because he knew that he, and everyone else on Sweet Briar Ranch, would work as hard as they could to make things work.

Part of that was getting people to come and book stays on their dude ranch. And if that meant that he had to go to the dude ranch competition with Carna, then he would.

"You can make sure she knows I'm driving, and I call the shots." He wasn't going to be henpecked the whole way there and back by some woman he could barely stand, and if he recalled correctly, Carna had always been bossy.

Smith chuckled. "She was a bossy little thing, wasn't she?"

"She must have been if that's the thing the both of us recall the most about her."

"You know, you don't want to be judged by your ten-year-old self, so maybe, and this is just a suggestion, you should give her the benefit of the doubt as well."

That made sense, and Smith was right. He had matured a lot since he hung out with Smith and Carna back when he was a kid.

Regardless, he'd learned that when he let his guard down, things usually went south.

"I guess you'll have to prove that to me. After all, my first experience with her in more than a decade was her letting the chickens out."

Smith pushed off the pole post, laughing and shaking his head. "I believe what she said about Billy. After all, you and I both know he's not a regular steer."

"You know it. I'm pretty much immune to Billy."

"What's that verse about pride going before a fall?" Smith asked as he started walking toward the barn door.

"It's not pride, man. It's just facts."

They were talking about Billy's penchant for being a matchmaking steer. The other men on the ranch, the guys who used to be on his crew, had all fallen and gotten married over the last few years. Miller alone had resisted love's pull and was the sole remaining bachelor.

And he had every intention of staying that way. He hadn't been joking to Smith about liking his space. Mostly because he didn't like to be bossed around, and while he didn't have a problem sharing, he also didn't mind having things to himself. To him, the sacrifices a man had to make when he got married were enough to negate the benefits.

"You know, there was a time when I would have agreed with you, but... Billy's presence usually means something's going down. If you're serious about wanting to stay single, I'd watch your step." Smith flashed him an amused glance before he walked out of the barn.

Miller unhooked the lead from Walker and led him back into the stall, noting that he wasn't limping nearly as bad as he had been the day before.

"I know, boy, you're going to be just fine. And so am I."

Chapter 3

Carna moved away from Miller and started toward the house.

Annoyed that her childhood nemesis was going to be, apparently, front and center at her new home.

Maybe she could talk to Smith and see if he could find a job for her somewhere far, far away from Miller.

Knowing her brother, he'd probably laugh and assign them something to do together.

She would have to make sure that she didn't mention that she didn't want to be around Miller.

There were some kids playing in the yard who waved at her as she came, but they must have been used to seeing company, because they didn't run over.

Posey whined a little, because there were several dogs running around as well.

But Carna didn't allow Posey to run over. And the other dogs seemed to be like the children and used to visitors.

Dogs, kids, chickens, and the Highland steer. It made for an interesting welcoming committee.

As she stepped up onto the porch, a voice called through the open screen door, "Come on in! We're up to our elbows in doing lunch packs right now, so just bring yourself on in."

Carna grinned a little, liking the casual hospitality, and opened the door.

"Come on back, we're in the kitchen!" a voice called.

She walked back to the kitchen, where two ladies stood at the table with several children around them, some cutting up vegetables, some packaging those vegetables in aluminum foil, and one little girl seemed to have the sole job of ripping sheets of aluminum foil off the roll. She was very specific about how big they were and did her job slowly and methodically and, from Carna's perspective, very well.

The kitchen smelled delicious, like there was something cooking in the oven. It wasn't the vegetables, which were not cooked, creating that scent.

"I think I want to stay here," Carna said, not joking. Of course, she was planning on staying, but the place seemed so welcoming, so friendly and busy, and it smelled delicious. Why would she not want to stay?

"That's the reaction we want to have from our guests," the woman who had called her into the kitchen said. "But I think you might be Carna, Smith's sister?"

"Yes." Carna thought to hold her hand out, but the lady was busy cutting onions, and she didn't want to make her stop. Several tears ran down her cheeks, which Carna assumed was from the pungent aroma of the onions.

"We've been watching for you, since Smith said you'd be arriving any day now. Nothing like giving a lady a little lead time," the second woman said. Then she smiled as she carefully folded up the aluminum foil, matching the edges and leaving a neat little packet after she folded the top down and tucked up the sides.

"I'm Piper, and this is Darby. She lives here, and I spend most of my time here, although my husband and I and our seven, going to be eight," she patted her stomach, "children sleep at our house just outside of Sweet Water."

"So nice to meet you. Those must have been some of yours outside," Carna said, indicating the children that had been playing with the dogs.

"I think they're a little of everyone's," Darby said with a laugh. "And this isn't even all of us. Which probably is a good thing, since I think if you had to meet us all at once, you'd be a little over-whelmed."

"I'm feeling a little overwhelmed as it is," Carna said, but then she had to add, "but in a good way. It feels very friendly and relaxed here. And I wasn't joking about not wanting to leave."

"Oh good, it's nice to have a little feedback from your first impression," Piper said as she carefully put an exact amount of potatoes, green peppers, onions, and mushrooms in the package before she gave it to Darby to fold up.

"Is there anything I can do to help?" Carna asked, not liking to stand and watch while it was obvious that everyone was as busy as they could be.

"If you could cut the onions, that would be great. Or if you prefer to put the vegetables on the aluminum foil, that would be fine, too. It's the onions that no one wants to do. So I end up doing both." Piper spoke as she went back to chopping onions.

"I'd be happy to chop the onions," Carna said, knowing that the new person should start at the bottom of the totem pole.

But the ladies had been so welcoming, never questioning her, but giving her a job and making her feel right at home.

"It's okay if I wash my hands first?"

"Please do, and then, this is my favorite knife, but there are others in the drawer if you have a different style that suits you."

Darby laughed and said, "Piper is so picky about her knife."

"It just feels comfortable in my hand," Piper said.

"That's crazy. Have you ever heard of someone who has a favorite knife?" Darby asked, laughing.

"It's perfectly normal to have a favorite knife, isn't it?" Piper asked, looking at Carna, who dried her hands on a towel.

"Well, I suppose. I don't have a favorite knife in the kitchen, but I do have a favorite pocketknife. And no other pocketknife fits my hand just the way that one does. I've actually tried to get a spare, just in case something happens to it, but nothing feels right."

"See!" Piper exclaimed, pointing a piece of pepper at Darby. "I told you!"

"Somehow I've managed to be in the kitchen with two of the craziest women in the world. Having a favorite knife." Darby shook her head.

Carna laughed, and just like that, she felt like family. Piper introduced her to two of the children who were helping them, Alice and Ingrid, saying that her oldest, Lucas, was out helping Gideon, her husband. Something with the cattle.

They talked a little about how they met their husbands and how they ended up working on the farm, and Carna listened, interested. She'd heard her brother Smith talking about the men who were now married to the ladies beside her.

She had never dreamed that this would happen to her, and she found it ironic that her life turned out this way. She had expected to be on her grandparents' farm in New Hampshire for the rest of her life, and now somehow she ended up in North Dakota with what seemed like her brother's whole crew.

"And what brings you out here?" Piper asked, when they finished talking about her kids and how Gideon had helped to put an addition on their home, and how she broke her leg, and how they somehow managed to fall in love after they decided to get married, which was crazy in Carna's opinion.

She'd never heard of anything like that.

But there was no question that Piper looked happy, and Darby did too, although Darby didn't have six kids. Just two. Although, she claimed they were working on a third.

"Well, I never expected to be out here," she started, unsure of exactly how much she wanted to say. But not really wanting to hold anything back. The ladies had been so sweet and welcoming to her, she wanted to return the favor. She felt like they were people who she could trust, even though she hadn't known them for very long. "My dream had always been to live on my grandparents' farm and take it over from them eventually. But it was so far in debt that we just couldn't do it. And both of them needed help as they grew older, and I somehow needed to pay for their care. I ended up having to sell the farm. That was...hard."

The ladies had both become sober, and Carna missed the jovial atmosphere that had been in the air.

"I'm sorry. I didn't mean to be a wet blanket."

"No. I know all about how it is when you have dreams and plans and hopes and everything just comes crashing down," Piper said. "That happened to me when my husband died."

"Gideon died?" Carna said immediately, because she thought they were just talking about him.

"No. My first husband. That's why Gideon had to put the addition on. I guess maybe I skimmed over that, because I didn't want to bore you with a big, long story, but I had six kids, and I was trying to support us all by cutting hair, and we were living in a two-bedroom home. I slept on the couch, because there just wasn't enough room for all of us." She shook her head and lifted her shoulder. "Anyway. It was not what I had planned. For sure. But God has a way of taking things from us so He can give us something even better. I am a lot happier here on the farm than I was cutting hair, squished in a two-bedroom home with six kids. I sometimes have to pinch myself every day because I can't believe this is my life. I hope that same thing happens to you."

"I do too," Carna said, meaning it but not really believing that it would. That just didn't seem to be the way her life worked out. She got the short end of the stick all the time, while other people around her thrived. No matter how much work she did, and no matter how much effort she put into things, it just seemed like nothing she touched ever succeeded.

She didn't want to think negatively about it, but she couldn't argue with the facts. She just seemed destined to never be a success.

"You know, it's kind of funny we're talking about that, because I had a similar situation, where I had to sell a very successful catering business to protect my daughter. I ended up coming out here, just because I wanted to find her father, and while selling the business was so very difficult, God opened so many doors and gave me a better life than I ever expected. But I had to go through that hard time first. I guess like Piper, I really hope that's what's happening to you, you have to have the bottom fall out before you can rise."

"I hope so," Carna said, but she knew her words didn't sound convincing.

She focused on chopping the onions and not crying as the conversation around the table ebbed and flowed. The kids seemed to be as much of a part of it as anyone else and didn't seem to be afraid to contribute. She liked that the kids were confident with the adults around them and that they weren't shuffled outside to play so they wouldn't be underfoot and in the way.

In fact, the kids were treated like they were an integral part of what they were doing. It was impressive, and Carna made sure to say so.

"What are all these things for?" Carna finally asked, when the table was loaded with foil-wrapped packages, and they had almost all the vegetables chopped.

"Oh! That would be kind of helpful to know, wouldn't it?" Darby said with a smile. "You know we do the dude ranch, and these packages of vegetables go in a cooler so our guests can cook them over a fire. Or we'll cook them and serve them on Saturdays when we have a lot of day guests. They come out, check out the chickens and the calves and all the other things that are going on over in the guest area, and these are campfire vegetables—that's what we call them."

Carna had noticed that Darby was putting a mixture of spices over the top before she closed them, along with a couple pats of butter.

"I bet they're delicious."

"They're one of our most popular items," Piper said. And Darby smiled. The smile made Carna think.

"You said you used to own a catering business? Are these your original recipe?"

Darby grinned. "That's right. I tweaked it a few times, but this summer, I think I have it down pat. Pretty much everyone loves them. Although, of course some people pick out the onions, and some people pick out the mushrooms, because you just can't please everyone, but this at least seems to be the perfect mixture."

Carna had three more onions to chop when her phone rang.

"That's Smith's ringtone. I'd better get it," she said as she wiped her hands on a towel and stepped away from the table, pulling her phone out of her pocket and swiping on.

"Hey, sis, glad you got here okay."

"Yeah. I've been...put to work in the kitchen. Which really made me feel welcome. Much better than being relegated to a room to rest by myself."

"You mean Miller didn't make you feel welcome?" Carna opened her mouth to let Smith know what she thought of Miller's welcoming abilities, but he continued talking before she could speak. "Good to hear it. There's always work to do, so another body will be nothing but welcome. Speaking of, I have something I need to ask you. Do you mind coming out to the barn? I have some calves to feed, and I can talk to you while I'm doing that."

"No. I have three more onions to chop, and then I'll be right out."

"All right. Thanks, sis."

She hung up and shoved her phone back in her pocket.

"Smith asked me to head out to the barn when I'm done with the onions."

"You can go right now if you want to," Piper said. "I can get the last three."

"No. He's said it would be okay for me to finish up, and I wanted to ask about Posey anyway. I made her stay out on the porch, because I wasn't sure whether it'd be okay for her to play with the kids or not. She hasn't been around many, but she's never been aggressive."

"Sure. People, kids, dogs, and whatever, we all kinda hang together around here. So whatever works for you. She'll be fine. We just don't let animals in this house, since we cook in here."

"All right. Got it. I'm not sure where Smith is going to have me staying."

"I think he has a room in the loft above the barn." Piper mentioned that casually, and although it was a surprise to Carna, she figured she wouldn't mind.

"It will work for the summer, but there's no heat there other than space heaters," Darby added.

"That's fine. It works for me." She noticed a little bit of worry in Darby's voice, and she wondered if it had something to do with what they'd mentioned before about overextending their finances in order to grow as quickly as they needed to.

The idea made a fuse of fear spread in her belly. She knew all about finances and losing the farm because of struggling with them. She really didn't want to go from New Hampshire to North Dakota and face the same problem.

She would really love to not have to worry about finances for at least a little bit. Money worries could be so stressful.

But she didn't say anything, and neither did either of the other two ladies.

Either because the kids were there, or because it wasn't something they were going to talk about. Carna didn't know and didn't really care. If there were going to be financial issues, she was sure she'd find out about them soon enough.

Chapter 4

"The farm is struggling," Smith said without preamble. He scooped milk replacer out of the bin and carefully squeezed the cup to make a funnel so he could pour it into the bottle.

"Struggling?" Carna asked, trepidation making her stomach feel sour. Had she left one failing farm, just to set foot on another as it failed too?

"We saw so much opportunity, we had so many ideas and great avenues open to us that we overextended ourselves. The ranch is viable, and it's popular too. But we need to bring in a lot more income this summer, or we're not going to be able to pay our bills."

"All right. Can you tell me the good news now?"

Smith smiled. He turned the water off, then put his hand over the top of the bottle, and lifted it with his other hand, shaking it hard. "You're here."

"Is that the best news you have?"

"Pretty much. No pressure or anything."

"I'm not feeling any pressure. But I can't imagine how me coming could be the best news you have. I'm just one more mouth to feed." She was supposed to have room and board and two meals a day, as part of her employment package. The compensation wasn't much, but she was being provided a room, and she didn't need much. She was happy just having the opportunity to work on a farm again, even if it wasn't hers.

Her heart might be in New England, but she could learn to love this rugged North Dakota wilderness. Plus, farming was farming, whether it was in New England, or whether it was in the West.

"Well, I had an idea, and I've already talked to Miller about it."

"Miller?" She tried to keep the dismay out of her voice, but she didn't think she was quite successful.

"I need a second bottle," he said as he finished shaking the one he held.

She grabbed the cup that he'd thrown into the canister and sank it deep into the powdered milk replacer. The scent wafted up, and she breathed deep. That sweet smell always made her smile, and mixed with the scent of fresh hay, the steaming bodies of animals, and the surprisingly comfortable scent of manure, it made her feel at home, even if she was two thousand miles from the home of her heart.

"I know. He's not any happier about that than I'm sure you will be, but you guys are our best hope."

"If Miller and I are your best hope, things are a lot worse than what I thought they might be."

Smith didn't even laugh. Not surprising, since Smith wasn't exactly known for his easy laughter or a quick sense of humor.

Although, she had noticed a definite change in him, from the few minutes she spent with him. He seemed more relaxed than he had since she knew him growing up. It had to be because of his wife, and that marriage agreed with him.

At least marriage to the right woman.

"I probably can't exaggerate how desperately we need you to come through for us, but I also don't want to make you nervous. I'll just say, I signed you guys up for the couples category at a three-day dude ranch competition next week. There will be a lot of spectators at that show, and the better you guys do, the more chance we have of being completely booked for the summer. That's the goal. If we can do that, we'll scrape by this winter, and I think we should burst open next spring."

"And if we aren't full this summer?"

"We're going to need to sell over the winter. There's no way we can make it."

"How did this happen?" she asked, although she knew. Unexpected expenses were every day in farming. A tractor broke down, and repairs could run into the tens of thousands of dollars, depending on what it was. She ought to know, she'd seen the bills. Animals could be lost, and bills could be higher than expected, building repairs, maintenance, the cost of fuel, and the volatile cost of fertilizer and seed and spray. All of those things combined to wreak havoc on a farmer's pocketbook and on their budget.

"Never mind. I know exactly how it could."

"I figured you probably did."

Smith had been in touch with her, and he'd offered more than once to come out, but she knew he had issues of his own to deal with, plus, being that he was newly married, she didn't want to strain their relationship with the financial issues in New Hampshire, which always seemed to make relationships worse.

Plus, she had known, almost from the beginning, that there had been no hope for salvaging their grandparents' farm. She hadn't wanted to drag Smith down too.

He could have invested money into it, but it would have been money that would have been lost forever, and now, she had the ranch to fall back on because he hadn't gone down with the farm in New Hampshire.

"You know, you might be better off getting a different couple, one who actually likes each other, to do the competition. I mean, aren't there lots of couples on the ranch?" She tried to sound diplomatic as her hand covered the top of the bottle and she shook it as hard as she could, tilting the bottle down to get the milk replacer that liked to stick in the corners of the bottle.

"It's always more exciting if you have two people who aren't married. And if they're not a couple, but there are sparks flying between them, that makes it more compelling."

She stopped shaking and blinked at her brother. He was older than she was, and they hadn't been exceptionally close growing up, but they'd been close enough for her to know she didn't get along with his friend Miller.

But the words that had just come out of his mouth were not words that she would expect from her taciturn and un-emotional brother.

"Since when did you become an expert on romance? Or relationships? Or emotions? Whatever that remark was meant to be."

He grinned. "Abrielle said it. She was the one who suggested that you two would be perfect. I happened to mention that the two of you fought like cats and dogs growing up, and she said that would be perfect for the competition. As long as you two can be civil to each other, I have a tendency to agree with her. She usually knows what she's talking about."

Carna gritted her teeth as she offered the bottle to the hungry calf in the pen beside the one Smith was already feeding.

She wanted to like Abrielle, but she didn't appreciate being stuck with someone she couldn't stand. And someone who was rude. Someone who was almost sure to make her cry, as much as she hated crying.

"I'm sure that probably works in most cases. But Miller and I actually can't stand each other, and so it probably won't work in ours. Because, a lot of times people pretend to not like each other when they actually do, but that's not what's going on with Miller and me. You know that the feelings are real."

"And our need for a couple to do the couples competition at the dude ranch show is real as well. It's just not as exciting when a couple who's already married are doing it. I'm sorry, but you're really the best hope we have. Not to mention, everyone else has family and responsibilities here. You just got here, so you are the most expendable. Not that we're not depending on you to pull your share here, because we actually really need help."

That made Carna feel a little bit better. And actually, the idea that she could help save the ranch was a really great one. The problem was, she didn't want to help save the ranch with Miller.

"Aren't there solo competitions?" she asked as the calf greedily sucked, milk foam forming at his mouth.

"There are, but the couples competition is always the most popular. And it's the one where we have the best shot. You wouldn't believe how talented some of the people are who actually partici- pate in these things."

"A lot of winning is luck," she murmured, smiling at the calf whose little brown eyes rolled back in complete enjoyment as his tail wagged furiously back and forth.

"I don't want to depend on luck. I want to send the people I think have the best chance of winning, and that's you and Miller."

Carna closed her mouth. She'd come out to help. If the ranch needed her, she would do it and she would do it without complaining, even if that meant working with Miller. As much as she disliked the idea.

Chapter 5

Do you want to make an offer?

June sat on the porch swing, looking at her phone. The evening air had cooled off as the sun had gone down, and she pulled her sweater more tightly around her.

Lifting her eyes, she looked off in the distance at the brilliant oranges and reds as they faded into pastel pinks and blues the further up in the sky her eyes went.

The first stars of the evening had come out, and they twinkled in the distance.

Winking and blinking and smiling at her. Seeming to be the total opposite of what her mood was.

Contemplative and serious.

Did she want to make an offer on the house she looked at earlier today?

It had been the fourth house that her realtor had taken her to see. There had been nothing wrong with the first three. She just hadn't moved in time, and they'd sold before she made a decision about whether or not she wanted to make an offer.

Her husband had cheated, he'd lied to her on an almost daily basis, he'd neglected her their entire marriage, and she'd spent it alone.

The swing rocked a little, and her foot trailed on the floor gently.

She was alone now. Watching the sun go down on a late evening in late spring in beautiful North Dakota.

She loved her town of Sweet Water, loved her friends and neighbors, but in the evening, when the sun was going down, when she was done with her busy day and wanted to unwind, she did it alone.

She ate supper alone. Ate breakfast alone, ate lunch alone. She went shopping alone. She went to church alone. She went to visit her grandchildren alone. Traveled alone. She went to doctors' appointments and fought cancer alone.

There really wasn't anything she did with her husband, unless it had to do with his job and him needing her to help him. Even those types of things had gotten fewer and further between.

A deep sadness washed over her. How much of her life had she wasted alone?

Back when she was young, she dreamed of building a lifetime relationship with her lifetime love. Creating the type of relationship that could only be built by years, decades of time spent together, of raising a family together, buying a house, living life together.

She had no idea when she got married that she was going to be doing all of those things alone. The relationship she thought she would have at the age she was was nonexistent.

The sadness, so deep it created a physical ache in her chest, pushed down.

She couldn't even look for a companion. She was married. Married but alone. Which surely was worse than being single and being alone.

It was a deeper loneliness, a loneliness that came from knowing that the person who had vowed to spend their life with her preferred to be anywhere but with her.

She felt an almost physical longing for companionship, for someone to hold her hand and sit beside her, to smile with, to do all the mundane things that married couples did together. Like sitting on the front porch and watching the sunset.

She swallowed, her throat tight because of the pressure in her chest.

She hated the self-pity that enveloped her, and she tried to shake it off.

I need truth in order to fight the feelings that want to drag me down.

Being alone all her life didn't mean it was wasted. It had been an opportunity to grow close to the Lord. If she had a husband who wanted to be with her, she wouldn't have had as much time to read her Bible. She wouldn't have had as much time to pray. She wouldn't have had the great need to depend on God, since her husband hadn't been around to depend on.

Wayne had not been with her when she'd been at the emergency room the seven or eight times she'd gone with each of her children.

She'd done it by herself. God and her. And they'd made it through.

Middle-of-the-night coughing spells, high fevers that wouldn't break, phone calls from the principal, bills she wasn't sure how she was going to pay, friends that turned out to not be friends at all, when each of her children left the nest...

She faced all of their situations, and thousands more, by herself.

That had made her a stronger person. Stronger in the sense that God's strength was what was upholding her and not a human relationship where she depended on her husband to take care of her.

She was confident and strong and had her security placed firmly in God's loving hands.

Maybe instead of feeling bad for herself, she should thank her husband for neglecting her, since if he had paid attention to her, loved her in word and deed, she wouldn't have clung so tightly to the Lord.

Still, God had made humans with an intrinsic need to be matched to a person of the opposite sex. To get married and create a family together, to love each other, to support each other. Life wasn't meant to be lived alone. Man wasn't meant to be alone. He was meant to have a partner.

So was woman.

But wasn't that God's will? Was it God's will for her to be married to someone who only thought of himself? God could have taken Wayne at any time, but He'd allowed him to stay in their marriage, knowing that that was what she needed.

She didn't need a husband who loved her, who cared for her, who lived to see her smile, and laughed and enjoyed spending time with her. For her to be sad and upset that she didn't have that was the same as her saying that God didn't know what He was doing when He allowed it.

The sad feeling eased a bit as she reminded herself that God was in control, and if He wanted for her to have all of the things she longed for, He would make sure she got them. If He didn't, it meant she didn't need them and they weren't best for her.

The idea still made her a little sad, but it helped to remember where the focus needed to be, not on herself and what she didn't have, but on God and what she could do for Him.

As if on cue, headlights flashed, and her husband pulled into the drive.

As always, a little nervous stress slithered down her backbone.

And despite the fact that she knew from decades of experience that today would be no different, despite knowing he'd cheated and lied, there was still a small hope that he would get out of the truck and greet her like he missed her.

The door slammed, his footsteps crunched on the gravel, and she watched his outline as he moved across the walk and came up the stairs.

"Good evening, Wayne," she said easily.

"You're still up?" he asked, looking over as though surprised to see her.

"It was a pretty sunset." He didn't say anything, and his footsteps sounded on the porch as he walked toward the door. "Would you like me to cook you something for supper?"

"I ate hours ago."

Of course he had. She used to keep supper warm for him, and then she'd be discouraged when he only ate a couple of bites, figuring he probably ate somewhere before he came home.

She'd given up cooking supper for anyone but herself when her daughter moved out, the last one to leave the nest.

"Would you like to come out and sit for a bit?" she asked, even though she knew he wouldn't.

"I'll be out. I have some things I need to do inside first."

When she was younger, for decades, that would have gotten her hopes up. She would have believed him when he said he was coming back out, no matter how many times he lied.

Now, she knew it for what it was, his way of saying no. When he didn't really want to say no, he lied to make it easier.

She kept her mouth closed, swallowing against the hurt and the loneliness and the nagging voice that told her that she didn't have to stay. He cheated on her, and God had given her an out.

The door opened, his footsteps sounded, and then it closed behind him.

She thought again about the last text she'd received.

Did she want to make an offer? Did she want to leave the hopes and dreams that she'd had since she was a young lady, embarking on what she thought would be the biggest adventure of her life? She had expected it to be hard, but she hadn't expected it to be lonely, and she definitely hadn't expected to do it by herself.

Pulling her phone out of her pocket, she held it in her hand for just a moment.

Lord? If You want me to stay, I'll stay.

She'd been saying that to Him for a long time, years, since she found out about her husband's infidelity.

God never seemed to answer her, never seemed to give her clear direction. Maybe that was why she hesitated putting offers on houses.

The temptation to go somewhere else, to relocate to a beach town, or a cabin in the woods, or somewhere cute and cozy and solitary, was strong. After all, she was used to being alone.

But she didn't want to leave her children, didn't want to leave her family, didn't want to leave the town that she loved and lived in for so many years.

She didn't even really want to leave her husband. Didn't want to give up on her dreams and admit to failure.

Fingering her phone, she knew she could leave. She could leave without getting divorced. She could walk out but not file; she didn't have to do everything all at once.

It would be nice to think that walking out would give him a jolt that would wake him up and make him realize that if he didn't change, he was going to lose what he had, but she wasn't so naïve as to believe that. In Wayne's eyes, nothing was ever his fault. Everything was always someone else's fault, and he never did anything wrong.

This wouldn't be any different. He wouldn't recognize that there was any problem on his part. He would simply blame everything on her, even if he had to make stuff up. He could make even the most egregious lie sound like the truth.

Not that she ever wanted to lie, but his was a talent she almost envied at times.

She couldn't even tell a white lie without sounding as guilty as sin.

Not that she wanted to get away with lying, but...he could say the most outrageous things, say them with such confidence and absolute sincerity, that anyone listening to him would believe him.

She believed him at times. Even after he'd lied to her over and over, she still fell for them.

For years. Although, not anymore. Now, when he said something, she had a tendency to ignore it. Or at least keep herself from getting excited.

Picking up her phone, the screen flared to life, and she swept up. It recognized her face, then her texting app came up.

She paused, her thumbs poised over the screen. It had been forty-five minutes since Wayne walked inside, promising to come back out. He wasn't going to. He'd probably taken a shower and sat down in front of the TV, unless he was on the phone with one of his friends.

Taking a deep breath, pushing the deep sadness that seemed to fill up the inside of her away, she allowed her fingers to move over the keypad.

Yes. Let's make an offer.

Chapter 6

Carna walked along the fence, looking at the small herd of mares and foals that were in the pasture.

Smith had told her she could spend the rest of the afternoon walking around getting used to the place. In the morning, she would report to the kitchen at the main house, and he would be there to tell her what to do, or he'd text her by 7 AM.

She was eager to get to work but also interested in what went on at the farm, figuring it was important to get to know the layout.

Smith had apologized, saying that they were busy, and he couldn't spare someone to show her the ropes.

She had offered to start working right away, but he'd asked her to familiarize herself with the places that she could.

The mares grazed contentedly, the grass higher than their heads as they buried them in the lush greenness.

Their foals, long legged and spindly, ran in circles around them, never venturing far from their mothers' sides.

She was curious to know how old they were, since none of them seemed to want to go more than ten or fifteen feet away from their dams.

They were curious and cute, and she stopped, putting one foot on the bottom rail of the fence and leaning her forearms over the top. On the farm in New Hampshire, they hadn't had many horses. Horses were a luxury that cost money, and they hadn't had any spare money for luxuries.

Out here, she figured horses were more a part of the workforce.

They did mention trail rides, both overnight and day trips, as well as herding cattle, branding, and working them.

She knew ATVs were used as well, but horses still played a big part.

Smith didn't go into a lot of details, just said that they had been breeding a little on the side, since some of the men on the ranch were interested.

As she watched, down on the far end of the pasture, a man walked to the gate, opened it, and slipped inside.

He had a small halter in his hands and lead rope coiled over his shoulder.

Pretty sure it was Miller, Carna was tempted to walk away. But she held still and shushed Posey as the dog lifted her head from where she lay at Carna's feet, growling low in her throat.

Miller's dog lay at the gate, and he walked in without him.

He seemed to want a particular mare, since he walked slowly, with no discernible purpose, other than his meandering gait took him to a pretty palomino, with golden hair and a flowing cream-colored mane and tail.

Her foal, a slightly lighter shade of gold, almost a caramel color, with the same light mane and tail, lifted his head, retreating behind his dam as the strange man drew closer.

Carna admired the soft, easy way Miller walked. Slowly, gently, but with no timidity.

It would take a lot of patience to work with the newborns, as everything seemed to scare them.

But Miller's smooth movements never turned jerky, and if he was annoyed that the foal ran from him, she couldn't tell.

He petted the mom for a little bit, until the foal couldn't help his curiosity, and his little nose peeked out from behind the side of his mom's big body.

Carna smiled. He looked so cute and inquisitive as he walked on four stiff legs toward the strange human.

Miller's hands moved from the mare's head down her neck and across her ribs, coming within a few inches of the foal, but he didn't try to touch him.

The foal moved a little closer, stretching his neck out as though trying to catch a whiff of Miller while standing as far away from him as he could.

So smoothly, she almost missed it, Miller's hands went from the dam to the foal, though he hardly seemed to notice as Miller ran his hand down the stubby mane and across the short back.

The touch did not bother the baby. As one hand continued to stroke along his rib cage, the other carefully positioned the halter he held and slipped it over the slender nose.

He must have done it a million times before, because he had him hooked within several seconds, with the lead rope attached.

He hooked a second lead to the mom, then wrapped the first lead around the baby's rear. Carna supposed that was so the rope would tug on his back end and not his head as he led him along.

With the mom in one hand, the baby in the other, Miller walked slowly back toward the gate, opening it with his foot as he led mom and baby through.

Turning them around was a little bit difficult, and Carna was tempted to jog the two hundred yards to where he was to give him a hand.

But he hadn't seemed to notice her, and they weren't exactly best friends or even casual friends.

She wasn't sure what to term their relationship. Maybe grudging acceptance, with no true likability, although even that sounded a little too friendly to describe whatever passed for a relationship between Miller and her.

Regardless, he got them turned, got the gate shut and fastened, and with the mom's lead in one hand, and the baby, still with the lead wrapped around his rear, in the other, he led them toward the barn.

It was a side of Miller she didn't usually get to see.

Normally he was making fun of her, picking, and laughing. Never in a mean way, at least nothing that she took as mean. Just in the way that let her know that she was the little sister and always would be.

Maybe that's what irritated her so much. She wanted to be recognized for the woman she was and not teased for the little girl she used to be. Who wanted to have their past mistakes thrown up in their face all the time?

Who wanted a nickname like Tater Tot?

Instead of letting it roll off her back, she somehow always found herself hitting him back as hard as she could. It was like a competition between them that she couldn't quite control and didn't really want to be a part of, but couldn't seem to escape.

That wasn't exactly a good excuse, but it was the best she could come up with. Miller was probably a nice guy. Most people she knew liked him, she probably should too. Except... Liking him was almost like admitting defeat.

And she didn't like to lose.

Carna tried to put Miller out of her head as she turned from the fence and walked along the dirt road that ran between two pasture fields. The field on the other side held cattle, which she could see grazing in the distance.

The dude ranch wasn't the only thing that Smith and his friends were into on the farm. They did crop dusting, ran several hundred head of cattle, and now had the horses they were breeding as well.

The dude ranch went along with that, for folks to come out and stay on the genuine working ranch.

She could understand the appeal. If she didn't work on a farm, it would be nice to visit one.

Even the chickens that were mostly Darby's responsibility, gathering eggs, milking the goats, and seeing the ducks, geese, and rabbits would be fun. Especially for children.

The goats were kept in a small enclosed area off to the side, and as she walked around, Carna even saw a building with a small enclosure that held some hogs. She didn't have much experience with pigs, and she found them the most fascinating after the horses.

One sow had a litter of what looked to be eight or twelve piglets running around her. It was impossible to count, because they were never still. Until they all piled on top of each other, in a giant heap, and went to sleep.

Even then, there were noses and tails and snouts sticking everywhere, and it still was impossible to count.

Still, they were cute, and Carna stood and watched them for a while.

Finally, her rumbling stomach and the fading daylight told her that it was time for her to check out her apartment.

It was above the stables, and she'd been putting off going to it, because she didn't want to run into Miller again.

Figuring that he had plenty of time to do whatever it was he was going to do with the mare and foal in the stables, she got her bearings, figured out which building housed the stables, and went in the opposite end from where she talked with Smith and where Miller had led the mare and foal.

The stables were quiet and dark, although she could hear some rustling and figured there were horses in at least some of the stalls.

Wondering if it was going to affect the way her apartment smelled, living over-top of horse stalls, she patted Posey on the head and said, "Come on. Let's go see where our new home sweet home is."

It was a little bit depressing to think that this might be where she ended up for the rest of her life.

She loved the idea of working on the farm, of being around her brother, of getting to know Darby and the other ladies, that had all seemed really nice, but... She wanted to own something her-self, not work for someone else for the rest of her life.

Reminding herself to be grateful that she had a roof over her head, and with

Posey's cold nose touching the back of her hand, she remembered to thank the Lord for her faithful dog too. She grabbed her bag, which she had set at the bottom of the steps earlier when she talked to Smith, and climbed the stairs.

Smith had said the apartment opened into a shared kitchen. At the back of the kitchen was a door for the shared bath which, in addition to a shower and toilet, held the washer and dryer.

On the right-hand side of the kitchen was a door with a lock which would be her room.

On the left-hand side of the kitchen was another door with a lock which would be a different tenant's room.

If there was ever someone living in the room on the left-hand side, they would share the kitchen and bath with her.

Smith hadn't mentioned whether there was anyone living in the second apartment or not, which made Carna think that most likely there wasn't anyone.

Smith was really good about warning her about things like that.

She opened the door to the kitchen, which was unlocked, and found it to be exactly as Smith had described.

There was a small area with counter space, refrigerator, stove, microwave, and a coffee pot front and center.

There was also a small table with two chairs along the side.

At the back was a door which Carna assumed was the bathroom.

She turned toward the right immediately, seeing the key that Smith had said would be on the counter, sitting exactly where he said it would be. She picked it up, unlocked the door, and walked into a bedroom that was larger than what she expected.

There were clean sheets sitting folded on a bare mattress and two pillows waiting for their pillowcases.

There was a comfortable chair, a lamp, and a small table with the chair.

A largish window overlooked the backside of the property, where grass waved in the wind.

All in all, it felt cozy and perfect.

Posey whined as Carna set down her small bag and walked back toward the door.

"Hold on. I'll get you a little bit of water."

Her own stomach rumbled. But she didn't have any groceries, and she wouldn't be going to town anytime soon.

Still, hopeful that there might be something edible, she opened the cupboards which were mostly bare, except for a package of sugar that was unopened and a can of coffee.

Priorities.

She grinned a little as she opened the refrigerator as a matter of course, not expecting to find anything.

But a plate covered in plastic wrap sat on the top shelf.

She recognized the stuffed peppers they'd had for lunch and smiled.

Darby or Piper must have taken pity on her and brought her some food for this evening.

Or most likely, they sent one of their children over with food.

Carna wasn't going to dwell on how it happened, she was just grateful that it did.

Pulling the food out, she carefully divided it in half, putting her half in the microwave and scraping Posey's half on a plate and setting it on the floor.

Posey gulped it down gratefully, licking the plate clean. She'd gone over to a corner to lie down by the time the microwave beeped, signaling that Carna's was done.

So much for having a dinner companion.

Grabbing her food out of the microwave, she walked to the small table and sat down. She was tempted to just take it to her room, but she figured she'd probably be spending enough time in her room, and the kitchen was cozy and bright.

Plus, she'd need to use the bathroom and take a shower anyway.

She'd just lifted her head after saying a short prayer, when footsteps sounded on the stairs, which caused Carna to tilt her head. Was someone coming to see her?

Maybe Smith had tomorrow's assignment and wanted to give it to her before he went to bed.

But when the door opened, it wasn't Smith.

Miller, dusty and dirty, holding his hat in one hand, walked in, closing the door and taking two steps toward the counter before he looked over and saw her sitting at the table.

His eyes narrowed. Obviously he wasn't happy to see her there, but then they dropped to the table, and his brows drew together.

"Did you steal my supper?"

Chapter 7

Miller stood in the middle of the small kitchen, disbelief causing him to stay rooted to the ground.

That, and maybe the fact that Carna was actually there, in the kitchen, too.

He hadn't given the possibility a thought. She was Smith's little sister, and he figured that she would have a place at the big house.

Maybe she hadn't wanted one, although he was almost positive that if she had known that he stayed above the stables, she would have stayed anywhere else.

Still, he was pretty sure that was his supper sitting in front of her, and he was starving.

His irritation was most likely amplified by the fact that it discombobulated him to find her there. This was his home. His sanctuary.

For now anyway, although he'd saved enough to start building his own house.

He just lacked the motivation. What was the point of living in a great big house all by himself?

He certainly didn't want to do that.

The small bedroom, kitchen, and bath of his current apartment suited him just fine.

Until Tater Tot had invaded his space.

"It didn't have your name on it," she said defensively. Then she lifted her chin. "Everyone knows that if something is yours, you label it clearly so that your roommates don't accidentally take it. Sorry about your luck, Ducky Doo Doo."

"Everyone doesn't know that. Whenever you're not sharing a room with anyone, you don't need to do that. How was I supposed to know you were going to invade my space today?"

His words were more of a growl than what he meant them to be, but it was annoying that she just plopped down and made herself at home, taking food out of the refrigerator and eating it.

It was true that he didn't have his name on it, but he didn't know he needed to.

"If you're going to be that upset about it, I can share it with you." She gave a smug smile, probably thinking that he wouldn't take her up on it.

She underestimated how hungry he was.

"All right. Share." He lifted a brow, challenging her, until she looked away.

Then he walked to the cupboard, grabbed a plate and a fork, and walked back.

"Are you serious?" she asked, looking at her plate, where her half-eaten stuffed peppers sat, and then at his and the obvious expectation that she was going to share with him.

The other choice he had was to walk across the barnyard, through the yard, and knock on the house door, begging for more leftovers from lunch.

He hated doing that.

He didn't mind grabbing some leftovers and taking them with him. Darby and the other ladies claimed it was a help, since something had to be done with them.

But to bother them in the evening after everyone was done working for the day, and they might be eating supper together, or spending family time together, the few precious moments that they had to spend, and there he would be interrupting them.

That's why he had moved out and lived above the stables. So they could have some privacy without him constantly un-derfoot.

He had hated it and felt like he was intruding when one of his buddies had gotten married and he was still hanging around.

He wouldn't want that for himself, after he got married.

He'd want time alone with his wife.

"You're really going to make me share?" she asked, looking at him like he had just asked her to do something illegal, rather than politely requesting that she share food that was already his.

"I'm not asking you to share, I'm of-fering to share with you. Whatever you keep is me being gracious to you."

He wanted to set the record straight. He was not being a jerk about this. He could take the whole thing.

She looked down at her dog, who had had her eye on him the entire time he'd been there.

He left Pepper downstairs. Pepper wasn't exactly his dog, but he seemed to have been adopted.

But Pepper didn't want to go upstairs, content to lie down and guard the door.

That made things easier for him to clean, and he was fine with that.

Her dog, on the other hand... He couldn't even remember what its name was, if he'd even heard it.

He almost mentioned that there was dog food and a water bowl downstairs in the tack room, but he didn't.

She could get her own dog food. Except, he hated the thought of her dog going hungry.

While he'd been thinking that, Carna had slowly moved to divide what was left of her pepper in half.

She did it thoughtfully, and before she scraped it on his plate, she held it up.

"Does that look like half?" she asked, with no friendliness in her tone at all.

It almost made Miller smile. She acted so put out. But the food was his.

He didn't allow anything resembling a smile to cross his face. After all, he was getting about a quarter of the supper that he should have had.

"Well, that's equal, but you already ate half of it. So I should have a larger share."

"I shared with my dog." Again her words were defensive, and she gave him a look under her lashes that should have caught his hair on fire.

He didn't reach up to check, even though he didn't have quite as much hair to spare as he used to.

"What you do with your half is your business. Unless I'm supposed to bring food home and share it with you and your dog?"

"So you're the kind of person who would starve a poor, defenseless little animal. I should have known. Actually, I think I did know, Ducky."

"All right, Tater Tot. You don't need to be mean. You know I would never starve an animal. However, I would never steal someone's stuff either."

"I didn't steal anything."

"I think we've already established the fact that you did. You knew I lived here, you knew that anything that was in here was mine."

"Actually, I did not know you lived here. And I assumed that Darby, or Piper, or someone else had brought food up for me, knowing that I would need something since I didn't have any groceries. I had no idea that you were going to barge in, invade my privacy, and demand my supper."

"I'm not demanding your supper. I'm demanding mine."

She was so annoying. She acted like she thought she was right, when any sane person could understand that he was the one who was right. He was the one who was being kind by not demanding that she fork over all the food.

"It's gross. I can't believe you'd want food that I've already slobbered all over. I think I might have sneezed on it too. Just saying."

"I don't care. I'm hungry, and it's food."

He snatched the plate as soon as she had filled it and grabbed his hat from where he'd thrown it on the counter.

Then he stomped to his room, closing the door behind him and wondering what he'd done with the key.

He never used it, since no one else had lived in the other room as long as he'd been there.

When they built the stables, they built the rooms overtop so that hired hands would have a place to stay, and it ended up that he, as the only unmarried owner of the ranch, had moved into one. It had been more than sufficient for him, and he lived there quite comfortably for almost a year.

It got a little chilly in the winter, with only a space heater for heat, but he couldn't complain.

At least he couldn't complain up until now. Now, he felt like he had a lot to complain about, considering that Tater Tot was stealing food, dirtying up his plates, and would probably expect him to wash the dishes.

Annoying.

Chapter 8

"Do you hear people screaming?" Abrielle asked, sitting on the side of the bed, brushing her hair.

Smith looked over at her affectionately.

Who would have thought when he first moved to Sweet Water, North Dakota, that he would end up married to the woman who was squatting at his aunt's house?

Certainly not him.

He wouldn't have thought that they would have built Sweet Briar Ranch into what it was today, either.

New houses, newborns, couples from his crew in the Air Force, and so much fun and laughter and excitement and plans.

So much that they overextended and borrowed more than they should have.

They needed to be successful, and now. He hated that pressure, but he also felt confident that he and his crew could do it. They would all work as hard as they could, doing whatever was necessary.

And there was some comfort in the idea that if they failed, they failed together. He liked that too.

Regardless, he tried not to think about those things after he hung up his hat for the night. Even if it was late when he got home, that still meant the bills and the worries and the problems of the day got hung up with it, and he had uninterrupted time with his wife and their two, almost three children.

Abrielle rubbed a hand over her stomach and looked up at him. "I asked you a question."

"I'm sorry. I got distracted by watching you brush your hair. You know I love that."

She did, which was why she sat on the edge of the bed and did it, rather than doing it in the bathroom like she used to.

There was just something about seeing his wife with her hair down, her nightgown on, and sitting in his bed that made whatever problems he had during the day completely disappear.

"Smith. Focus." Her smile said she wasn't annoyed, and even though her words were short, they were said softly as she turned her head to look at him.

"Right. Do I hear people screaming? No. I don't. Carna has not killed Miller yet. Or else if she did, she taped his mouth shut first. I think that's a good thing."

"This is not funny. Those two could really hurt each other."

"Those two are long past the time where they realize they're both attracted to each other, and they need to do something about it. Especially if they're going to be here on the ranch. We're all going to be miserable if we have to watch them pick and poke at each other and then dance away before they can actually figure out that they're picking and poking because they like each other."

"I think you took everything I said and swallowed it, hook, line, and sinker."

"Are you saying you have me hooked? Because that's right." He put both hands on the bed and looked at his wife as she set her brush down on the stand.

"I don't think there was ever any question about how hooked I was." He grinned, wolfish. "The question is what you're going to do about it." He put a knee on the bed, slowly, stalking her.

It didn't scare her in the least. In fact, she grinned and turned toward him.

"Smith. We're talking about Miller and Carna. I'm thinking that someone needs to go check on them, to make sure that both of them are still alive."

"We can deal with the bodies in the morning." He moved another four inches closer toward her. "Now. Can we stop talking about bodies, unless we're talking about yours. Then, I'm definitely interested."

"Oh. You want to feel the baby move? She was pretty active just a bit ago, but I think she's gone back to sleep."

"I would love to feel the baby move anytime. But that wasn't what I was thinking."

She knew it. She was just messing with him, and he liked it. Liked that she teased him and smiled with him, and didn't have a problem having lighter moments. Work on the farm could be hard, consuming, and could wear a person down. It could make someone think that everything had to be completely serious all the time. But he didn't want that. He wanted to be able to have fun times with his wife no matter what was going on around them. She totally got that.

"Good. Then you're thinking that you need to go and check on your friend. I know we can do the bodies in the morning, but it's best to deal with things as they happen, not put them off until later."

"Miller can take care of himself."

He reached her, growling just a bit as he put his head down on her neck, rubbing his lips over the corner of her jaw and feeling her shiver.

"Do you think it's going to work?"

"I think so. Just give me a few minutes, and I'll let you know for sure."

"Not you, doofus. I'm talking about Miller and Carna. Do you think putting them up above the stables together is going to help them see that they are actually quite attracted to each other?"

"Considering that you'd never met Carna and haven't seen the way they act together, I'm totally trusting the fact that you know what you're talking about and that the way they treat each other is actually attraction, rather than true animosity, as I've always believed. Now, as for me, and the way I feel about you, there is no confusion. And if you want to keep the light on, I'm fine with that."

"It is so hard to get you to focus," she said, brushing his temple with her lips before she got off the bed to go shut off the light.

He grinned. She'd been warned; now he just needed to get her back in here and have her stop talking about his friend and sister, because he wasn't the slightest bit interested in either one of them right now.

"I'm focused. It's not hard at all to get me to focus. All you have to do is sit there and brush your hair. Actually, you don't even have to do that."

She lifted the covers, and the bed sagged a bit as she climbed in.

She came directly to his arms, as he had known she would, and he was waiting for her.

Knowing Abrielle, she truly was concerned about Miller and Carna, and although he felt her concern, he knew it was totally misplaced. Neither one of them was going to hurt the other. Neither one of them was going to be so upset with the other that anything was going to happen. If anything, they were going to ignore each other and still never get together. That was why they had come up with the idea of partnering them for the competition.

But knowing Abrielle the way he did, she was going to need to have her mind set at rest about them before she was going to be interested in anything else. And he was definitely hoping to get her interested in something else.

"Don't worry about Miller. He can hold his own. And he's got a level head on his shoulders; he's not going to do anything at all to Carna."

"You don't think that it was dangerous of us to not tell them that they were going to be together? I kept listening for screaming coming from the stables, and I didn't hear anything, but I can see me being really upset when...someone ends up in my house who doesn't belong in it."

She kissed the bottom of his jaw, and he could feel her smile.

He returned it. After all, that had happened to them. "I'm guessing Carna is probably out there with her masking tape right now, dividing the kitchen in two."

"Are you ever going to let me live that down?" she asked, chuckling at his gentle teasing.

After all, that's exactly what she had done.

"Miller is probably threatening to throw away all of her bras. Can you imagine?"

He laughed outright. "He just wants to get his hands on some lingerie." Maybe that's not exactly what he wanted to get his hands on, but Smith left it alone. He didn't want to think about Miller's hands, he wanted to think about his own.

"Speaking of hands, this feels pretty good," he murmured, causing Abrielle to giggle.

Her own hands went exploring, and he hoped they were done talking about his friend and his sister. Not that he didn't love his buddy and his sister, but a man didn't want to take either one of those to bed with him.

"Smith. Do you think we need to do more to get them together?"

He paused, his hand in a really nice warm spot.

He didn't want to placate his wife just to get what he wanted, so he stopped what he was doing and forced himself to think about his friend. Again.

"I can make them work together tomorrow. We can tell them that they need to practice for the competition. Or we can tell them they just need to get to know each other so they can work well in the competition. I know by morning you can have a million excuses thought up that I can give that will make it sound like it's perfectly reasonable for me to assign him to do something with her tomorrow. Does that sound good?"

"Yes." Her hand moved a little lower, and he shifted up just slightly, not wanting to impede her in any way, whatever she was planning. "Thanks for listening to me. For taking me seriously. For helping."

"I'm not sure why it's so important for you to have everybody matched and married, but if it makes you happy, it makes me happy. I think you know that."

"There are a few other things I know that make you happy as well," she said, and while he could hear the smile in her voice, there was a husky note there, too, which he really appreciated.

It meant that, while he was going to have to assign his friend to work with his sister tomorrow, coming up with some hopefully good excuses, for now, he and his wife weren't going to be talking for a while. And he appreciated that even more.

Chapter 9

"Can't you find someone else to babysit her?"

Smith gave Miller a look, but Miller didn't back down.

He didn't want to do anything with Tater Tot. The woman was too annoying by far. Not to mention, she'd grown up a lot since he knew her when she was a teen, and she was a lot more appealing now than she had been then.

He wasn't used to disliking someone he found so attractive.

He decided last night after he finished his food, checked to make sure the coast was clear before he grabbed a shower, making sure to lock the door, and then stood at the window, hands on the sash, looking out at the wide North Dakota sky, that it was okay to realize that Tater Tot was grown-up.

What was not okay was having anything but animosity toward her.

Maybe a little bit of condescending affection, but definitely not anything that spoke of his attraction.

That would be embarrassing. She didn't want it, since she saw him as her annoying older brother's best friend and as a pain in her rear. An annoying teenage brat.

She probably didn't realize that he had grown up too. He certainly wasn't the kid he used to be. Even he could admit that he'd been a jerk at times. Wasn't everyone when they were young? Young and dumb. That certainly described him.

He would expect her to notice that he'd grown up, but not like he'd noticed her. So he just needed to play it cool. Which meant for the most part staying away from her.

It had seemed like a good plan, until 5:30 this morning, with coffee cup in hand, he'd gone down to the stables to scoop out some food for his dog and see what kind of day it was going to be.

Smith had the same idea, and they met halfway between the house and the stables, coffee in hand, dressed to work.

"It's not about babysitting, and you know it. No one has time on this ranch for babysitting. Plus, you're not giving her credit. She was in New Hampshire for years on my grandparents' farm. She knows farming."

"She knows Eastern farming. That's a good bit different than what we do here."

"I'm not going to argue with you about that. But the basics of farming is the same everywhere. No money, no time, and constant work. She can work. And you know it."

Miller couldn't argue with that. Even when they'd been kids, no one had been able to outwork Carna. She set goals for herself, and she accomplished them like knocking pins off the windowsill. One at a time, in a deliberate manner.

It was one of the things he admired about her, even as he teased and picked on her.

Regardless, he didn't want to give any ground, because he was desperate to not have to be with her. He'd just decided last night that that was his only hope, and now, Smith wanted them to spend all day together.

"She showed herself around yesterday, but only because you were busy with Fancy and her baby. You can give her a quick tour of the place, explain to her what our goals and thoughts are for everything, so we can all be pulling in the same direction. Then, the inside of the bunkhouse needs to be painted. As soon as that's done, and a couple of other little odds and ends, we'll be ready to start hosting people overnight. That's the big goal."

"She can just go right to the painting. She can have that done in a day or two, and she doesn't need me to hold her hand."

"She needs you to show her around. And then with the two of you doing it together, it'll get done twice as fast." Smith didn't fool Miller with his casual stance. He wasn't quite the commander of their Air Force years, but the man expected to be obeyed.

Still, Miller couldn't help arguing, because he didn't understand why he needed to be with Carna.

"You guys are going to be doing the competition together, and it's good for you to get reacquainted with each other and to learn to work together. Thus, the best thing that you can do is to practice. Develop a camaraderie that the other competitors don't have. Have you forgotten that we need the income that we're hoping to generate from the interest that you get from winning the competition?"

"I haven't forgotten." He really hadn't, but he didn't want to have to have all the weight of the responsibility for the ranch resting on how he worked with someone he couldn't stand.

He supposed trying to say that to Smith wouldn't get him anywhere. Because Smith would say, and he would be right, that all of them needed to do things they didn't want to do. All of them needed to work with people who might not be their favorite. All of them needed to give a little, in order for the ranch to be successful.

He certainly didn't want to be the reason that everything they had done went up in smoke.

"It will be over in a few weeks. After that, we can assign Carna to one end of the ranch, and we'll assign you to the other. But in the meantime, I want the two of you working together, all day long, every day, so you can go into that competition with the very best advantage that you can have." Smith smacked him on the shoulder, nodded his head, and then strolled away.

Pepper whined a little but didn't get up from where he laid at his feet.

Miller wasn't quite sure why Pepper had chosen him out of all the other people in the ranch to hang out with, but ever since someone had dropped the stray dog off on the driveway, Pepper had bonded to Miller and typically didn't let him out of his sight.

Considering that Carna ran around with her dog trotting at her heels, he hoped that Pepper and whatever the shaggy beast's name was would get along.

Their conversation seemed to be over, and that was probably just as well. It was an argument that he wasn't going to win.

Smith, while not a dictator, was the undisputed leader, the person who always gave the orders for what needed to be done.

He certainly took advice and suggestions from everyone and considered each one carefully. After all, they all brought different experiences to the table, and Smith wouldn't be a good leader if he ignored the fact.

Irritated, but knowing he had no choice, Miller started walking back toward the stable.

Sleeping Beauty probably wouldn't be up for another couple of hours, so he'd have a little time to work with the horses before he needed to escort her highness around the farm.

Billy, that steer that usually hung out in Sweet Water, moseyed across the path in front of him.

He stopped to scratch his back, working his way up to the ears and under the neck, the spot Billy really enjoyed.

"I think we spend a little bit too much time together when I know your sweet spots, old boy," he said while scratching.

Billy must be five or six years old. He'd been hanging around Sweet Water for years, and after the first few months when no one claimed him, everyone had been taking care of him. He developed quite a reputation for himself, although Miller considered himself immune to whatever matchmaking powers Billy had. After all, he knew Billy for years and hadn't gotten matched with anyone.

Of course, Billy typically spent most of his time in town, which was just fine with Miller. He didn't need to be matched in order to be happy.

Although, he supposed there was something to be said about having a wife waking up beside a fellow every morning.

Someone to talk to. Someone to build a house for.

He had the money in his account, just hadn't felt a great need to break away from the community at the ranch and build a big empty house to knock around by himself in.

"Just leave me alone, Billy. I'm perfectly happy in my little spot above the stable, as long as someone can keep their grubby fingers off of my food and stay out of my way."

"Are you still complaining about that? And to Billy no less." Carna's voice cut through the stillness of the morning.

It didn't exactly make the morning worse, it...made it a little bit more exciting, if Miller was going to be honest.

"Take your time. You got out of bed before noon. That's new."

"When you were sixteen, you slept in longer than that." She raised her brows at him. "Am I right to think that you still do, Ducky?"

He didn't allow the way she said his nickname to make him smile. It wasn't something he would allow anyone else in the world to call him, but coming from Carna, it always sounded...not cute exactly but like something he had earned.

Which was ridiculous. He knew the nickname should irritate him to pieces, and he allowed Carna to think it did, but it didn't bother him at all. He kind of liked it.

On the other hand, she hated Tater Tot and had told him that multiple times when they were younger. So he made a point of using it every time he saw her.

"I'm not sixteen anymore. I'm sure you haven't noticed, but some of us have grown up. Matured. Become adults." He gave Billy one more pat on the head. "And some of us haven't." He started to walk away. "Oh, by the way. Smith said you're supposed to spend the day with me. I'm going to stack the fifty-pound bags of horse feed that're sitting on the pallet in the stables, so you can go ahead and put on your back brace or whatever it is that you need and come give me a hand."

He wasn't expecting her to lift fifty-pound sacks of feed, but he needed to let her know that she was supposed to be following him around all day, and even more importantly, she needed to understand that it was going to be her following him, not the other way around.

"I don't know why you'd make something like that up. Smith knows better than to assign me to chase your tail all day. I can't think of anything that smells worse."

"That's weird. I haven't noticed that you've run around sniffing behind me. Good to know." He shook his head. "Some people are so kinky," he muttered under his breath as he walked away. She could go talk to Smith if she wanted to; maybe she could get him to change his mind.

He wasn't going to let her know that he'd been unsuccessful. He didn't want her to know that he didn't want to be around her at all. Knowing the way Car-na was, she'd make sure that every time he turned around, she was standing in his face.

That was the last thing he wanted.

Chapter 10

"**S**tay right there. I'll be right back out." Carna put her finger up in front of Posey's nose, making sure the dog understood before she opened the door and walked in the farmhouse, calling out, "Good morning."

She didn't say it too loud, just in case the children were still sleeping.

"Good morning. Come on in!" Abrielle, working in the kitchen, stuck her head through the doorway. "Carna! Good to see you. Is everything okay?"

"Everything's fine. I was going to thank you for sticking the food in the fridge yesterday, but Miller said it was his. Still, I figured I'd bring the dish back."

"You don't have to wash his dishes."

"Oh, I didn't. It was washed and sitting in the draining board this morning when I got up. So I figured I'd bring it. I assumed it belongs in your kitchen."

"It does. Miller's very good at washing them, but he's not always great at returning them. Are you two getting along okay?" Abrielle bit her lip like she wasn't sure whether she should ask that question or not, or maybe she was just nervous about the answer.

Probably both.

"Fine. We never really liked each other, and that hasn't changed. He already tried to ruin my day by telling me I was supposed to work with him today. Which I know is ridiculous. Smith would never do that to me."

She wasn't entirely sure that was true. Smith, after all, was a typical older brother and enjoyed giving his sister a hard time. But even Smith couldn't be that mean.

"Oh... I think that the idea is that you two can work together and develop a camaraderie that will help you during the competition." Abrielle wiped her hands on a dish towel and took the clean plates from Carna. "We have a lot riding on the competition, and we're really hoping that the two of you can pull off some amazing feat of not just winning it but engendering enough interest that people will book and we'll have a full summer schedule for the rest of the year."

"That's a lot of responsibility, but I know I'm going to do my best. Miller probably will too." She wanted to say something more about him. That maybe they could hope that he wouldn't screw up or something like that, but Miller had always been dependable; no matter how much she hadn't liked him, and no matter how much he had teased her, he'd always done what he was expected to do and had done it to the best of his ability.

She admired that in anyone, and she couldn't not give Miller the credit that was his due. Even if she had to give it begrudgingly.

"Oh, I have no doubt that the two of you are going to do your very best. And I think that will be more than enough for us to come up with the people that we need, plus we've got some advertisements going out as well. Kenni has been working on some marketing, and I saw that there were about fifteen or twenty new emails, although I wanted to get breakfast over before I sat down at the computer and started answering them."

"That's great! Maybe we'll get some bookings."

"Yeah. And I think that's what Smith was going to have you two doing, painting the inside of the bunkhouse. Just in case we get those bookings, it needs to be done."

"Miller had said something about unloading some feed."

"Well, whatever Miller is doing is what you're supposed to be doing too. I know that you two aren't the best of friends, but maybe spending a little bit of time together will help you to like each other more?" Abrielle looked hopeful, and Carna hated to disappoint her, but there was no way Miller was going to like her a little more. Although he couldn't like her any less.

"I think probably the more time we spend together, the more chance there is going to be that there will be a murder on the property. Maybe that will bring in tourists, at least around Halloween if you're doing any kind of haunt-ed house/ghost trails type thing."

Abrielle shivered. "I know they're popu-lar, but I don't think I want to have any-thing to do with anything that's haunt-ed." She didn't say anything more, and Carna let it be.

She wasn't overly fond of dabbling in the spirit world either, but some people really got a charge out of those types of things, and it was hard not to want to profit from that.

"All right, if you're sure that's what Smith wants, I guess I'll go find Miller and attach myself to his hip."

"Don't get too close. At least not until you guys start liking each other a little more."

Carna laughed and walked back out of the kitchen. There was zero chance of her learning to like Miller a little more.

As she thought that, the picture of him working with the mare and foal yesterday in the pasture came into her mind. It wasn't just that he looked good doing it, although he had, with his wide shoulders and worn work boots, and his hat pulled low over his face, his jaw square and serious, his hands gentle. It was probably the gentle hands that did it for her. But it was his patience, the way he didn't hurry them but waited for them to do what he wanted them to, without force.

She wasn't even sure she had that kind of patience. She admired it in other people. Loved it in a man. And there, that was probably her problem more than anything else.

She found herself admiring him.

And the man could make her laugh. She tried to hide it, but every time he called her Tater Tot, she wanted to grin.

It was a childish nickname, but she thought it was cute, and no one else called her anything but exactly her name. It was fun to have someone who had shared history with her and called her something that the rest of the world didn't understand.

She liked it but had to hide the fact that she did, because she was pretty sure if Miller figured out that she liked it, he'd stop calling her that. Because his main purpose in life still seemed to be to annoy her as much as he could.

Posey jumped up from her position by the door as Carna walked out, and they went down the porch steps together.

Carna stopped for a moment, since Billy stood right in the middle of the path to the barn. She reached out, scratching the steer and musing over the fact that everyone seemed to think he was a matchmaker.

That was so funny. The idea that people put stock in such ridiculous things. But that's the way it went in small towns. People, desperate for tourism dollars, would say pretty much anything.

Still, it wasn't Billy's fault that they made so much of him, so she petted him for a little bit more before she straightened and moseyed out to the barn.

It wasn't even six o'clock yet, so it wasn't that she felt like she needed to hit the ground running to put in a full day's work.

Smith hadn't given her any specific hours. He actually hadn't given her anything specific other than what she heard rumors of today, working with Miller and participating in the competition.

Beyond that, he hadn't said how long he expected her to work or even what her days off would be.

He probably figured that she knew that farming was a seven-days-a-week, twenty-four-hours-a-day job, and people just pitched in where they needed to. He also knew her well enough to know that she would put everything she had into it. Knew he could depend on getting a full day's work out of her.

Regardless, she figured she probably ought to talk to someone, because she needed to go get groceries. Unless she did what Miller obviously did, which was take leftovers from lunch and eat them for supper.

That seemed to be just as good as any-thing else and probably a smart idea. Maybe they could divide the refrigerator in two, where he got the top shelf and she got the two bottom shelves.

However she suggested it happen, he would probably complain that she didn't divide it fairly. Maybe he could do that.

Maybe he had some masking tape, and they could divide it directly down the middle.

That seemed like a good idea, and she made a note to either ask him or just do it, then label the left side Miller, since his apartment was on the left side, and the right side Carna. Surely he could understand that.

Entering the stables, she waited for her dog to go through before she closed the door behind her. Several horses nickered, and straw rustled.

A bag thumped, and she peered through the darkness to the far end where a figure worked in the shadows.

"Miller? I'm here."

"The feed is down here. You're not doing any good there, and I'm going to make a note to tell the boss that you were late."

"The boss didn't give me a starting time, so I can hardly be late."

"You're supposed to start when I do, and I started fifteen minutes ago, so you're late. Hopefully he'll dock your pay double, because if people aren't willing to pull their weight, they need to be let go."

"It's not that I'm not willing to pull my weight, I just didn't know what time you were starting. If you tell me, I'll be here."

"You saw me. We passed in the yard. You knew I was going to work, and you chose to continue to the house."

"Because I was taking the plate back that you stole from the kitchen."

"I didn't steal anything. I took food from the kitchen, which is perfectly within my right to do, but I understand that a thief like yourself would assume every-one else in the world is a thief as well. Sometimes it's hard to get out of your lit-tle bubble and realize that not everyone is exactly like you."

He thumped another bag of feed down on the pile that had been growing steadi-ly and didn't even look at her before he started back toward the skid.

He had it half unloaded, and she did feel bad. She didn't realize that he was going to start unloading feed at six o'clock in the morning.

When she worked on her grandparents' farm, they'd gone out to the barn at 4:30 to get started milking the cows although they didn't turn the pumps on until 5:30. It just took that long to get everything ready. That's if the cows came in. Every once in a while, in the summer especially, the cows were pretty happy out in the pasture and didn't bother to come down to be milked.

Normally they could call them, but it made things a little bit later. Of course, new calves, something that was broken, or they lost electricity and had to mess with the generator, or there was a host of other things that could cause them to be late.

In farming, something almost always happened every day.

She learned the one thing she could depend on was there was nothing she could depend on.

It seemed like a rather negative way to live, but it was the truth nonetheless.

It made a person rely completely on the Lord.

Thinking about New Hampshire got her mind off Miller, and she was almost smiling as she walked over to pick up a sack of feed.

Fifty pounds was a lot, almost half of what she weighed, and her arms were going to be Jell-O by the time they were done unloading it. But if it was the kind of work that she was going to be expected to do, there was no better time than the present to start getting used to it.

She walked over and hefted up a bag, Posey at her heels.

After she slapped the bag down on the pile, she told Posey to sit and stay.

"There's dog food in the tack room." Miller's words were clipped, short, and begrudging, like he didn't want to tell her but felt bad for her dog.

It made her mad, and she wanted to explain that she had been traveling as light as she could and hadn't wanted to haul a bunch of groceries onto the ranch when she wasn't sure where she was going to be staying or what kind of room she was going to have.

Of course she knew she needed to feed her dog, and she assumed that she was going to have time to grab some things from town. She wasn't entirely sure what kind of things the grocery store in Sweet Water had. Smith had told her that it had been growing a lot over the years and was much bigger than it used to be, but they still had to go to Rockerton for any kind of major shopping trip.

Still, as much as she wanted to ignore Miller and just work without talking to him, she wasn't going to make her dog suffer.

"Thanks," she said. "I'll work an extra thirty seconds at the end of the day, since I'm going to take thirty seconds off now to take my dog to the tack room."

"I'll hold you to that," Miller said, and he didn't crack a smile.

Jerk.

"Come on, Posey," she said, snapping her fingers at her dog to let her know that she didn't have to stay any longer.

"You call your dog Posey?" His words were condescending.

"I didn't name her." She didn't elaborate. He didn't deserve it. She wasn't going to give him any explanations, because she didn't know him and had zero desire to engage him in conversation or explain herself to him. Plus, he was going to hold her to those extra thirty seconds at the end of the day, and she didn't want to make it forty-five.

She almost rolled her eyes, but instead, she went to the tack room, helped Posey find the food, and left the door cracked as she walked away from her dog, hoping that her dog would stay, and she wouldn't have to stand there while she ate.

Posey didn't like to be out of her sight, which most of the time wasn't a problem. Anywhere Carna went on the farm, her dog went, too. Posey was great with other people, and she usually got along with other dogs, thankfully, since Miller's dog had been lying in a corner and Carna assumed that he followed him around all day too.

Coming back out, she started working immediately, without saying anything.

She supposed she owed him a thank you, but it could wait. She wasn't in any rush to give him more consideration than what he deserved. Any consideration seemed to be more than he deserved.

She was right, and by the time they had the last of the bags moved from the skid to the pile beside the tack room, her arms felt like they were going to fall off.

She wasn't sure whether she would have been able to carry one more bag.

Not to mention, her legs felt almost as bad.

Back on the farm in New Hampshire, there was a lot of work to do, but she didn't typically haul fifty-pound bags around.

"The paint is in the bunkhouse, and we're headed there next. Come on, Pepper," Miller said, not even stopping to take a break after he put the last sack down.

What was he, some kind of machine?

She wanted a drink at least.

"I thought you were supposed to show me around the farm?"

"If I have to. I thought you were supposed to show yourself around yesterday?"

"I walked around, and I saw everything, of course. But there was no one to explain to me what was going on. That would be helpful." It would also be helpful to have a little break. As much as she didn't want to stroll around the farm with Miller, she needed to give her arms a chance to rest, because there was no way she was going to start painting with the rubbery way they felt right now.

At least, she wasn't going to have to worry about getting out of shape.

Not that that had been her biggest concern in her life at any point anyway.

"All right. We'll take a quick tour starting here. This is the foaling barn. All the feed that we just unloaded is mare and foal feed. That's what we give the mares after they have their babies. It helps recondition them, especially if they've had a difficult pregnancy and delivery, as Fancy did right here." His voice softened as he stopped at Fancy's stall, and she stuck her head over the top of the door. "I already fed them. For today. That's what I do first thing when I get up."

"Before coffee, Ducky?" she asked, because she couldn't imagine jumping out of bed and running down to feed without even getting a little bit of coffee in her system first.

"I usually have my cup with me." His voice wasn't quite as begrudging as it had been, but he still didn't sound friendly.

She couldn't blame him. She didn't like working with him any more than he obviously liked working with her.

But as he talked, it occurred to her that it was silly for her to be upset with him. After all, it was hardly his fault that they were assigned to work with each other.

Her getting annoyed about it and taking it out on him was just as childish as him doing the same.

Chapter 11

Miller scratched the horse he called Fancy between the ears, and a little movement in the shadow reminded Carna that she had a foal.

Before she thought about it, she said, "This is the horse I saw you bringing in yesterday. She has a baby."

"A filly. Just a week old. I'm teaching her to lead with a halter. She's doing pretty good." There was a lot of affection in his voice as he spoke, which didn't surprise Carna, because she'd seen the way he handled them yesterday. He obviously loved them.

"She's shy," Carna said, unable to stop the smile that stole over her face as the little baby pranced behind her mom, peeking out before reaching forward like Carna had seen her do last night, then jerking back, using her mom's big body as a shield.

"We're working on that. She's going to be a pretty friendly one just like her mom. She's got a sweet personality."

"You love horses."

Maybe she shouldn't have said that, because the little smile that had ghosted across his face disappeared immediately.

"I told you I grew up and I'm not the same person I used to be."

"I don't think either of us are."

He didn't say anything to that, and she let it go as well. After all, it would be surprising if both of them still acted like teenagers. They had just spoken the obvious, but maybe they had both been assuming the worst of each other.

Miller moved on to the next stall. "This is Monday. She is due to foal any day. I've been keeping a close eye on her, and if you notice, there's a camera in her stall. I have it connected to an app on my phone, and I can check her day and night."

"Even in the dark?"

"We have a dim bulb on, above her, enough for me to see if she's up or down. This is a foaling stall. That's why it's so much bigger."

Miller's voice was once again brisk and businesslike, which suited Carna just fine. She didn't want to think about him as a man who loved horses and was patient, kind, and gentle. And funny.

She was already having enough trouble with him. He didn't need to endear himself to her any more.

Still, she couldn't help but look into the stall where Monday stood, looking fat and uncomfortable. "She looks like she can't wait to have it," she couldn't help but say, laughing a little.

To her surprise, he joined her in her laughter.

"She's a little late. We like to foal earlier in the spring, although it's nice to wait for warmer weather too. That way, the snow is melted and they can go outside."

"Why not wait until summer when it's nice and warm?"

"Well, first of all, there's the flies. And nice and warm is sometimes too hot. But also, typically horses turn one year old on January first of the year following the year they were born. So the later in the year they're born, the younger they actually are when they're considered one. It's a disadvantage all around. A horse born in July isn't as mature of a two-year-old as one born in February or March. So there's that, and then also at twenty years old, nine months could be the difference between nineteen and twenty, which doesn't sound like a lot, but it could affect the amount of money that you're able to get for them if you want to sell."

Carna couldn't believe he was taking the time to explain all that to her, and while she didn't exactly understand completely, it wasn't hard to figure out that the earlier in the year a foal was born, the better it was all around.

Whether she understood the finer points or not probably didn't matter currently, and in her experience, a lot of times things figured themselves out.

"Do you have any other mares that are going to foal this year?"

"We had five that have foaled already, and they're all bred back for next year. They should foal in April or early May.

We have two more plus Monday who have yet to foal. We'll breed those back as soon as we can, to try to get them to drop their babies a little bit earlier in the season next year."

"I see. How soon after they foal do you breed them?"

"Three weeks. If everything goes well."

She knew all about things going well. On the farm if a cow had trouble with her birth, or if she got infected afterward or twisted, she wouldn't bounce back right away. Even cows that gave a lot of milk sometimes didn't have a heat cycle for a month or even two after they freshened. It stood to reason that some horses were very similar.

Although, she heard from multiple people that horses and cattle were completely different in a lot of different areas.

"It's kind of funny how different horses are from cows. I have a lot of experience with cows, but I've always been told that horses are different."

"There are a lot of differences. Horses are a lot touchier for one. Which makes sense, because beef cows especially have been bred for their hardiness in calving. That's one of the main things people breed for, beyond marbling in the meat. And the ability to gain weight quickly at a young age. All of those are factors. But cows typically have their babies in the field with very little human intervention. Horses are completely different. We have them a little closer to us so we can intervene, and a horse that has speed or intelligence or quickness or an inbred sense of working cattle is valuable, even if they have trouble foaling. Typically, when we breed for one thing, you get negatives with your positives. That's just the way things go."

She thought about that for a bit, and she had to agree. Hens that laid a lot of eggs typically didn't sit on them to hatch them. Which was a positive in a lot of ways, unless they needed to raise babies.

Still, any time people tried to manipulate what God created, they often ended up with things that they didn't want in addition to the things they did.

It was interesting hearing it coming from Miller though. It gave a depth to his personality that she hadn't credited him for. She might have called him shallow and not very intelligent.

She would have been wrong.

He went down the rest of the stalls, stopping at each one that was occupied and taking his time telling her the name and a little bit about them.

"I thought you said there were five mares that already foaled. But Fancy is the only one in here that has a foal by her side. Or did I miss them?" she asked, after he'd shown her five or six more horses and told her that the rest of the stalls were empty.

"We have the mares and their foals out in the pasture behind the barn. It's a little bit bigger than the side pasture, and they have more room to run. I try to go out a few times a week and work with them. It's not entirely necessary. When we bring them in to brand them, we can break them without them being gentle, but I like to do things a little bit differently. I feel like you get a better horse. Although, ranch horses are not very good if they're in your pocket all the time."

"In your pocket?"

"Like a dog." He jerked his head at Posey who had followed them quietly the whole time they'd been walking around the stable.

"Pepper follows you," she said, feeling like he said there was something wrong with her dog.

"That's fine. With a dog. He'll stay when I tell him to and he'll come too."

"Mine will too," she said, still feeling defensive.

"I'm sure she will, Tater Tot. Don't get yourself all worked up. I'm just saying, you don't want that in a horse. Not in a ranch horse. They've got a job to do, and they need to remember that. They're not here for the kicks and giggles, at least most of them."

"When people come to the ranch and ride horses, they probably want one that is friendly and nice."

"That's true, and we have most of our riding horses in a different pasture. For the most part, they're easy to catch, some of them are old ranch horses, but some of them are just great horses that needed a home. As long as they're gentle and don't buck or do anything that's going to hurt one of our guests, they work for the trail rides."

"People want to ride the pretty ones though."

"Doesn't seem to matter what their personality is, because you're right. People are drawn to the flashy colors. So that does help."

"Do you prefer that?"

"To some extent. For the most part, the breeding that we've done is more for animals that we know will work on the ranch. It takes a lot of time to train a horse, but to buy one already trained costs a lot of money. Deuce has been helping us train our own, and that's something that most of us like to do, something we can do in our downtime."

"I noticed there was no TV in the kitchen or my bedroom."

"No one has time to watch TV," he said dismissively, like everyone knew that.

Back in New Hampshire, they didn't have a TV either, although that was not the norm. In the winter, the days were short and they often went to bed early, like they were catching up from all the work they did in harvest.

In the summer, they often worked in the garden and then sat on the porch snapping beans or shelling peas or husking corn in the evenings.

Sometimes they canned vegetables that night before they went to bed, and sometimes they'd do it in the morning directly after the milking while it was still cool.

Thinking about those days caused a wave of longing to wash over her.

"Hey. You pass out?" Miller asked as he lifted his hand up, almost as though he was going to catch her, before it dropped immediately back to his side.

"No. I'm fine." She pushed the thoughts of New Hampshire away. Those days were over, and she was starting a new life. She couldn't live in her memories.

"All right. Some of the horses you saw were ranch geldings. We keep them in so if we need to grab a horse quick, we don't have to go to the pasture and spend ten minutes trying to catch one. Sometimes the older horses can be a little wily. They know when we go out to get them, we're going to expect them to work. That just saves time."

"That makes sense. So are the ranch geldings in a different pasture?" she asked, burying the thoughts of New Hampshire and her grandparents. This was a new start, and even though things were wildly different here, more differ-ent than she had ever expected, they weren't completely unfamiliar. She was used to working around animals, and she was used to working hard. Just be-cause it looked a little different in North Dakota than it did in New Hampshire didn't mean she couldn't adjust and car-ry on.

Miller said a few more words and they mucked out a few stalls before they left the horse barn, with Carna and the dogs trailing at his heels.

Chapter 12

To Miller's surprise, the last two hours had gone by rather quickly. He hadn't minded showing Carna the horses, and she'd been a good help in cleaning out the stalls.

She seemed interested, even if he knew she didn't have much experience with horses.

He hadn't either until he'd come out to the ranch, but he'd been a quick learner. For him, working with horses had been natural, and he had fallen in love with everything they represented.

Still, he steeled himself as he walked out, unwilling to soften toward Carna. If she was interested in horses as well, he might end up working with her more instead of less. And he didn't want that.

Why would that be so bad?

The thought almost stopped him cold. He stumbled a little but picked up a step and continued to walk, hoping she didn't notice as she followed along behind.

Because she hated him. That's why it would be so bad. Except she hadn't been acting like she hated him. She'd almost been acting...like maybe she didn't want to be friends, but that maybe they could put the past behind them.

"Miller! Miller!" Eliza came running over, her camera wrapped around her neck, her advertising face on.

He managed to keep from groaning, although barely. He loved her, she was great, but she took her job as marketing director very seriously and was constantly trying to get the best pics to use in their marketing material. Miller understood how important that was, and he always did his best to accommodate, but he didn't want to get suckered into a picture when he was supposed to be working with Carna. He wanted to get whatever he needed to Doo Doone and over with.

"I just heard you two are going to be in the competition together! I want to get pictures of you guys that I can use as promotional materials, not only to send to the competition for them to use but for us on the ranch as well!" She smiled engagingly. "I know you guys are really busy. Everyone always is, but I was hoping that you would be able to go change quickly and wear matching outfits so I can get some good pics. And I really wanted to get them beside Billy, after all, you're doing the couples competition, and Billy is our matchmaking steer!"

She lifted her hands up, as though encompassing the entire ranch or maybe just Billy and the matchmaking idea. Whatever it was, she sounded way too excited for Miller's taste.

"I don't have anything that matches with her." He tried not to sound surly, but he was afraid he did.

"It's okay. Just wear the same color. Surely you both have blue shirts or something?" She looked hopefully between Carna and Miller.

Carna continued walking until she stopped just six inches or so in front of Miller. He figured that was probably a dominant tactic, one to show that she was just a little ahead of him.

It was annoying, but he didn't move.

"I have a red shirt, a green shirt, and two blue shirts. I can wear any one of them or this one which is kind of brown." She held up the arm to show the long-sleeved flannel she wore.

He noted she had some kind of shirt underneath that, and it was partially un-buttoned.

He was happy she didn't take it off. He didn't need to know what was under there.

"Miller? I know you have a blue shirt."

He looked down at the black T-shirt he was wearing.

"Black matches anything." He felt like an idiot for saying that, but he knew that much about style anyway.

"But I want to get the perfect shot, and it would be best if you guys could have at least the same color on, if not the same style. You do have a button-down, don't you, Miller?"

"I do. But it's going to be too hot today to wear it."

He wished he could keep from being so surly. He didn't want to give Eliza a hard time. She was only doing her job.

"I'll wear whatever I can, whatever complements him."

"Perfect. You two go change, figure out what you're wearing on the way. I'll grab Billy and get someone to give me a hand. Probably one of the kids. I'll get some hay bales set up back behind the barn." She pointed to the big barn, where they kept the dry hay and where they typically parked their equipment over the winter. It was basically a pole building, but they had a bunch of pole buildings, and they'd named that one the barn.

Eliza turned and hurried away, calling over to a group of kids who were outside playing by the corner of the house. Two adults were in the garden, and a couple of the older kids were there as well.

It was always nicer to work when it was cool out, before the heat of the day. So it wasn't surprising that so many people were out and about. That was probably why Eliza wanted to get the pictures done. That, or the angle of the sun. He didn't know. Pictures weren't exactly his thing. His phone could take them, but he typically didn't. Except for newborn foals. Every once in a while, he couldn't resist them.

"All right, what color are you going to wear?"

"Black," he said, without looking at Carna. The last thing he wanted to do was coordinate outfits with her.

"You could be at least a little bit agreeable," she snapped. Her patience was probably at an end. He hadn't exactly been the easiest person to work with all day, and he definitely owed her an apology. This was not the way he would want to be treated if he were new on someone's ranch, and it definitely wasn't the way he would normally treat someone.

"Red." His word was begrudged, but he figured he'd go upstairs, change, and work on his attitude.

"You had to pick the worst color, didn't you? You know I hate red. Man," she huffed, turning on her toes and walking away.

"What happened to, 'I'll do whatever he wants. He can pick the color.'" He mimicked her voice.

"I thought you'd be at least a little bit considerate," she threw over her shoulder, practically stomping back into the stables.

"So in other words, your word isn't any good?"

She whirled around, her finger up, her face pinched. "I don't appreciate that at all. I've never lied to you. And you know it. If you want red, I'll do red. You just know I hate that color."

He didn't know any such thing. Red was an okay color. It wasn't his favorite, but he had a red shirt, and he knew it was clean. That's why he chose that color. It had nothing to do with her.

"Ever since I came, ever since you saw me, you've done everything you can to make my life miserable. It's been a real trial and hardship just to be around you, and then you go and pull a stunt like this. Now I'm going to look ridiculous in the first promotional pictures that we're going to have, we're going to go to this couples thing, which is obviously going to be a lot different than the stuff that I'm used to doing, and you're going to make me as uncomfortable as I can possibly be. Could you be a bigger jerk?"

She stomped her foot, swinging back around and marching up the stairs.

She was kinda cute when she was angry.

But he wasn't so naïve as to think that she would appreciate hearing him say that right now. So he didn't.

He strolled into the stables, touching Fancy's head as he walked by her stall before he called, "Blue."

"Aargh!" She threw her hands up, grabbed the doorknob, and yanked.

She pulled a little too hard, or maybe she forgot how easily that door opened, because it flew open, smacked her on the head, then flew back shut.

"Ouch!" There was more muttering under her breath, although he didn't hear any profanity. Still, the muttering made him smile. Even as he cringed. That had to have hurt.

She yanked the door again, only this time she kept a hold of it, swung it wide, made sure her dog got through, and then slammed it shut.

Only, the door was light, and it probably didn't give her the satisfying slamming sound she wanted.

He could hear her stomping around even through the closed door. It made him smile.

Not that he had made her mad. He hated that, and he knew he owed her an apology, but still, seeing her so upset was...adorable. It hadn't happened too often.

Maybe it was just all the new things, or the idea that her picture was going to be plastered everywhere.

He was never super thrilled about it, but he'd gotten used to it. He wasn't on social media, so the first few times that Eliza had taken his picture and put it places, it had made him uncomfortable. But it was one of the sacrifices that had to be made in order to help the ranch be successful, and he hadn't really thought too much about it, just got used to it.

Maybe that was her problem. He could probably talk to her about it and tell her that he had felt the exact same way at one point.

But he felt like he'd destroyed their relationship to the point where he doubted she would listen to him say anything at this point.

Which was sad, because he really did want to try to ease her mind and help her.

Odd urges, especially considering he didn't even like her.

Did he?

She'd taken his teasing and his grumpiness with as much aplomb as anyone could be expected to. And she'd been up before dawn, expecting to work.

Normally he would never expect her to throw those heavy feed bags around. They probably weighed half as much as she did, but she hadn't complained about that at all either.

He had to admit a grudging respect for her. Especially since all he'd done was be as nasty to her as he could possibly be.

He made his way upstairs, with Pepper waiting for him at the bottom.

He opened the door with a good deal less force than what Carna had and walked in.

She was walking out of her room, buttoning up a red shirt.

"I said blue."

"You said red first. So that's what we're going to do."

"I changed my mind. I want blue now." His words were quiet but commanding. He worked to keep the smile off his face.

"Too bad. I'm wearing red."

"You're the one who said you were going to do whatever works for me. Blue works for me."

"Blue doesn't work for me. Red does," she said, her words coming out through gritted teeth.

"If we do red, we're not doing what works for me. We're doing what works for you." There might have been a little bit of heat in his words. He thought she was going to capitulate a lot easier.

"We can stand here and argue about it all day, or you can go change. If you wanted to change your mind, you should have done it before I got the shirt on."

"I'll go change into my blue shirt. If you're not changed into your blue shirt by the time I'm changed, I can go into your room and get it. I'll carry it to the photo site, and then I can have Eliza make you change there."

She pressed her lips together and stared at him, as though wondering whether or not he was going to do what he said he was going to do.

He admitted he could be a little stubborn at times, and he definitely felt his heels digging in right now. They were going to have their pictures taken in blue shirts, and that was the end of that.

Except, hadn't he just thought to himself that he was going to try to be nicer? Then here he was, the first opportunity God gave him to be nicer, and instead of being nicer, he was allowing his stubborn nature to take over and demanding his way again.

He hated it when he did that.

Still, pride was a hard thing to fight, and it was another five seconds before he said, "You know what. Let's do red."

He didn't wait for her reaction but walked into his room, not bothering to shut the door behind him, and grabbed his red button-down. He could put it overtop of his black T-shirt and then take it off as soon as they were done. By this afternoon, the button-down was going to be way too hot.

"Close the door, button it up, tuck it in the way it's supposed to be, and don't come out until you're done." She had her arms crossed over her chest, and she tapped one foot.

"The way you did?"

"I have mine tied in front. Unless you want to look like a girl and tie your shirt, you need to get it tucked in."

"And can you say that nicely?" he asked in the calmest voice he had, because her bossiness irritated him to the point where he wanted to go in and stand in front of her and take the T-shirt off and walk down without one.

Not that he would ever do such a thing, but the idea was tempting.

"Never mind." He grinned. "Yes, Tater Tot, I mean ma'am." He almost winked before he turned around and went back to his room. This time, he didn't come out until his shirt was on properly, tucked in, and he'd even grabbed his Sunday belt buckle. The one he only wore to church and the few times he went to town each year.

He thought about changing his cowboy boots into his fancy pair that he wore if he ever had to get dressed up and go to something like a wedding, but he decided that was too much.

Hopefully the pictures weren't supposed to show people who didn't actually look like they worked for a living.

Although in his experience, that's often what they wanted.

Still, other than grabbing his brand-new hat that he had sitting in the closet and had only worn twice, there wasn't much else he could do to change himself.

His jeans were clean, even if they did smell since he'd been working in the horse barn in them, but a picture wouldn't pick that up, so he was good to go.

"Do I look acceptable now?" he asked as he stepped out.

Carna hadn't moved much, although her arms weren't crossed over her chest anymore. She was down on one knee, petting her dog.

She straightened slowly.

"I suppose you'll do. Although, you'd look better if you had a day's worth of growth on your face."

Really? That kinda surprised him, but he tucked it away to think about later.

"I suppose you could donate some of your hair and we could get some glue," he said in a fake effort to appear accommodating.

"Yeah. That'll work. I'll get right on that."

"Hey," he said, reaching the door before she did and putting his hand on it but not opening it.

Forcing her to stop.

She looked up at him, her expression closed or maybe irritated.

One brow lifted.

"Sorry. I... I remember our animosity when we were younger, and I guess I kind of just assumed you didn't like me much. And I figured there wasn't much

I could do to change that. I guess... I wasn't very nice, and I'm sorry."

"You guess?" she said, lifting her brows clear to her hairline and throwing her jaw out. "There's no guessing. You were a jerk."

"You weren't exactly the nicest person in the world," he said, then he clamped his mouth shut. An apology was worthless if he threw insults at her the second the words were out of his mouth. "You know what. Never mind. I'm sorry. I was wrong. I did things wrong. I wasn't nice. And I hope you'll forgive me. I'll try to do better."

Maybe that worked to soften her just a little, because the rod that seemed to be shoved down her back eased just a bit.

"All right. I accept. I forgive you. And... You're right. I probably could have been nicer as well."

"Probably?" He didn't say anything else, just allowed her to think about it, and if she wanted to add something onto it, she could. After all, they both knew there was no probably about it, any more than there was any guessing about his.

"You're right. Thank you for the good example. I... I'm sorry. I'll try to be nicer too." She pursed her lips and looked down to the side before she looked back at him. "But I can still call you Ducky Doo Doo, right?"

"As long as I can call you Tater Tot," he returned, unwilling to tell her that he actually liked the nickname. As long as it was only her that was calling him that. He'd put a quick stop to it if anyone else started. But he didn't figure he had to worry about that.

Chapter 13

The pictures didn't turn out too bad.

In fact, Carna was kind of happy with them. Considering it was a spur-of-the-moment thing.

Eliza had been brilliant, and she had Alice and Amber helping her. Two of the kids that lived on the farms. There were so many kids running around, and people for that matter, that Carna figured she probably would never get all the names straight, but Amber and Alice had been helpful and mature, moving the props around, making sure that Billy was where he was supposed to be, and Billy himself had been an angel. Allowing them to set his feet where they wanted them, giving him a regal stance, and they'd even managed to make him look a little goofy, having him turn his head to look at them while they stood behind him with their backs to each other and their arms crossed, looking over their shoulders at each other.

That was probably her favorite picture, but they all had personality and fun as well as having an authentic ranch look.

As much as she hated the color red, it was probably the perfect color to go with the beige siding. The blue would not have stood out as well, and she was glad that they'd ended up using it. Not that she would admit that to Miller. Not under any circumstances. Except... They seemed to have called a truce. And he'd actually been...maybe not nice to her, but at least not brusque or downright rude.

They were finishing up the photo shoot, just a couple last shots, when Smith came striding around the corner of the barn.

"Are you guys almost finished up?"

"Just a couple more shots, but we can quit if you need them."

"Actually, I do. We have people who were vacationing in the area, and they scheduled a picnic trail ride for this afternoon. I know it's almost lunchtime, but if you two don't mind, I've got a crew out making hay, and two out spraying, and you guys are the only ones avail-able. I didn't want to turn down the business, especially since they're visiting here from New York City."

"That's no problem. We can do it right now."

Carna almost opened her mouth to protest. The man hadn't asked her what she wanted.

But her answer would have been the same, even though she resented the fact that he assumed that he could just speak for her. She wanted to tell him she had a mouth, and she could form her own answers.

She could just smile and feel warm and happy that he could read her mind, but that seemed like too much of a stretch of the truth.

Plus, she didn't want someone like Miller reading her mind.

Actually, someone like Miller...might be a good thing. He seemed like an upright man. He'd been an okay kid, but he'd grown up into a man with character. She actually wouldn't mind having a man like Miller. But not Miller himself. Because, while they seemed to have a sort of truce going on, she still wasn't sure she actually liked him. In fact, she was pretty sure she still didn't. She wanted to not like him.

Not that that made any sense at all.

"Come on, Posey." They'd actually gotten some cute pictures of the dogs as well, and Alice and Amber had somehow scrounged up some red bandannas and a red lead rope and halter for Billy.

The red in the picture did make everything pop, even if it was still her least favorite color in the entire world. After black.

"Thank you, guys. I really appreciate you taking time out to do this. I think these pictures turned out awesome. We can use them on our website and send a few on to the competition too. They're really striking. You guys make an awesome couple."

Carna had stopped and was smiling as Eliza talked, but on that last line, the one that she said almost as an afterthought, Carna caught her breath.

She and Miller did not make a couple, striking or otherwise.

Unless she missed her guess, Miller stumbled over that too.

She called, "You're welcome!" over her shoulder as she walked away, slightly behind Miller, and laughed a little.

He glanced over his shoulder, and his own eyes started to twinkle. "Awesome couple? That's rich."

"I know. Can you imagine? That is so ridiculous."

They laughed together as she fell into step beside him, their dogs at their heels, walking toward the stable.

Miller seemed to need a few more steps to compose himself, and Carna had to overcome the unusual desire to dissolve into a gaggle of giggles, but finally, he cleared his throat and said, "We'll saddle up a couple of ranch horses for ourselves, and then we'll go over to the pen, and I'll introduce you to the horses, show you where the tack is, and when the people come, the first thing we'll do is let them pick their horse, then the kitchen should have us a picnic ready, all we have to do is pick it up, and—"

"Excuse me."

He stopped and stared at her. "Yeah?"

"I've never ridden a horse."

His mouth opened. Then closed. Then opened again. "Right. You're from New Hampshire. I should have known."

"I'm from Ohio, the same as you. I just moved to New Hampshire after high school."

"Ohio, New Hampshire, it's pretty much the same thing. They don't use horses like we do out here." He sighed. "All right. Well, we don't exactly have time for a riding lesson today. And you heard Smith. There isn't anyone else. He always likes to send two guides. No matter how many people there are. Did he say how many?"

"I don't think he did. I think he just said a group. I'm willing to go. I'm just letting you know that I'm probably going to be more of a liability than a help."

"It's all right. As long as there are two people there representing the ranch, and we can present you as a new person, you can relate to anyone there who hasn't ridden before…" His voice trailed off, like he was still trying to put a positive spin on it.

She said what he probably was thinking. "They might all be seasoned riders."

"No. Smith said they were from New York City. They don't ride horses in New York City any more than they do in New Hampshire."

"Even out west, I'm sure there are people here who haven't ridden horses." She felt like she was lacking somehow. It was hardly her fault that she never had the opportunity to ride a horse. Where she came from, only rich people had horses. She didn't know anyone in her school, in her town, who actually rode horses on a regular basis. She doubted that Miller did either. It was only when he came out here that he actually got into it.

His eyes clouded, then cleared, as though he realized what she was saying. "I didn't mean to insult you. When I came out here, I didn't know much about horses either."

"I just feel like I'm lacking somehow. I wanted to be able to pull my weight right away, but it feels like there's so much to learn."

"You know most of the stuff. And you know farming isn't technical work, it's more just the willingness to work hard."

"I guess I'd rather ride a horse than drive a tractor," she said with a little bit of a smile. She'd driven tractors and skid loaders, but on the farm in New Hampshire, they bought most of their feed, so there wasn't too much work to do in the field, other than a few small hayfields to make every year. Cutting it, raking it, and bailing it into the big round bales.

She'd done it because it needed to be done. She supposed that was what Miller was saying now. It was just a matter of having the gumption to do it and having the willingness to put in the hours.

She had both.

"I don't think you have to drive a tractor around here if you don't want to.

There are plenty of other people. Usually we're not quite this shorthanded, but the spring hay season is the busiest, you know that."

She did. And she nodded.

They started to walk again, going past the house and coming to a fenced pasture.

"This pasture actually joins the bunkhouse on the other side. The office is over there, and that's where all the guests go. You probably saw the signs when you pulled in the driveway."

"Yes. That's where you tried to direct me to go when I got here."

"Right."

She didn't mean to rub it in. She probably should apologize, but he moved on, and she just tried to make sure that she had the foresight to not mention that again. She wasn't holding it against him.

Not really.

"So that's where they'll go. And we'll meet them over there. Right now, we'll grab a horse for me, one of the ones we have in the stalls I showed you this morning." He stopped for a minute. "You could probably ride the other one. He's not wild, and he listens well, but he's just trained to do a lot of things. If you accidentally touch him with your foot in the wrong way, he's going to start doing something you didn't intend for him to do. That's probably the only reason that I think it'd be better for you to ride one of the horses from the trail riding pen."

"All right. I don't want my horse to start doing a bunch of weird things. I'll probably fall off, if I don't panic first. Or maybe I'll fall off and panic at the same time."

"Panicking is never good, so try not to do that."

She'd mostly been kidding, but she nodded, since he seemed serious.

"Horses can pick up on the way you feel. Not all the time, and some are worse at it than others, but if you're scared, they might take advantage of it. So you want to try to have as much confidence as you can. And I can promise you, even though we do have a little bit of history together, I won't put you on a horse I think is going to hurt you."

He talked while he pulled the lead on one of the horses that were in a stall and pulled out a pretty brown horse.

"This is Sherlock. No, I didn't name him. He's a great ranch horse. He'll help us get the trail horses rounded up and pushed over to the other side." He tied him to a post as he talked. "I'll have you take the four-wheeler over and throw some feed in the trough, so once the horses see you, they'll go on through. Some of them can be a little bit tough to catch."

He'd mentioned that before, and she wasn't sure exactly what he meant, but she knew they didn't have a whole lot of time. The group was supposed to be there in less than an hour. So he didn't have time to teach her how to ride, and they definitely didn't have time to mess around trying to get horses that didn't want to be caught.

It was annoying that she wasn't a better help, but she tried to push that aside and listen while he explained what he was doing as he was tacking up.

He apologized for not taking more time, but he'd mentioned the time crunch, and he didn't have to say it twice. She understood.

Waving her hand, she said, "I understand we got people coming. You just do what you need to do, and I'll try to keep up. We can put some more time into this later, if you don't mind."

"We probably need to do it for the competition anyway, so we'll definitely be putting more time into it later. But thanks," he said, lifting one corner of his mouth and making her feel like she'd done something right. Even if it was just backing up and trying to stay out of the way.

Chapter 14

He should be a lot more upset than what he was. He had been paired with someone who had never ridden a horse, and now he was supposed to share the workload with her as they led a trail ride together.

But Miller couldn't find it in himself to be even a little bit annoyed.

Sure, he was going to end up doing the bulk of the work and the bulk of the instructions, but Carna was still willing to jump in and do anything, and he knew she would help him out however she could.

Plus, once he stopped being so antagonistic toward her, they seemed to be getting along rather well.

He'd actually almost enjoyed the photo shoot, for the first time ever. Normally those things were things he just suffered to get through. But the one today was almost fun.

"I'm almost finished tacking this old boy up. Grab that white bucket over there, and go over to the barrel on the left. Put two scoops of feed in it, and...you do know how to ride a four-wheeler, correct?"

Her cheeks heated again, which was cute. She might have grown up and wasn't the teenager that he used to know anymore, but she still looked young to him. Even though she had to be pushing thirty since he was a couple years older.

She rolled her eyes, but immediately she did what he told her to do, her dog at her heels.

He'd been a little concerned about the dog as well. Dogs who wouldn't listen could get in a lot of trouble on a ranch. Not only could they scare the livestock, bite a guest, rip the garbage apart, or potentially kill a baby goat or even chickens, but they could just be a nuisance.

Her dog was well-trained, and most of the time, he barely even knew she was there. Kind of like Pepper.

Pepper had grown on him, and he'd be offended if he decided to start hanging out with someone else. Although, he caught Pepper looking at Posey and Carna, and it made him feel like maybe he should give his dog a little bit more attention.

"I've gotten used to having you around, old boy. I wouldn't want you to cut out on me. Not now."

Pepper whined and wagged his tail slowly, looking up into his face as though trying to figure out what he was trying to tell him. He'd spent more than a few winter evenings teaching Pepper some basic commands, until he was fairly well trained and was a great companion to have around. Especially on a trail ride like this. He'd give them a little bit of warning if something seemed to be off.

Checking the weather on his phone and seeing that it wasn't supposed to rain until that evening, he made a mental note to not be late getting back. Typically, morning and afternoon trail rides lasted four hours each.

"I have two scoops in here," Carna said as she arrived carrying the bucket.

"You can grab the four-wheeler that's in the equipment shed. There's a green one and two blue ones. I think the green one should be on the end. Can you go get it and bring it over?"

"I sure can," she said, starting off with purpose. She had a farmer's walk. His mom had talked about that some as they'd been growing up in Ohio. They didn't live on a farm, but his mom had been raised on one, and his mom had always said that her parents had told her she walked like a farmer. He took that to mean it was a businesslike walk, no-non-sense, where a person didn't stop to think about swaying their hips or making themselves look cute, but they were walking to get where they were supposed to go to do what they were supposed to do. With purpose.

That was how Carna walked, and he had to admit, there was a certain appeal in that for him.

He stopped that thought and then remembered that there had been a truce declared between them. She wasn't acting like she hated him anymore. Maybe he could admire her a little. Not just her go-get-'em attitude, and her ability to work hard, but the way she looked as well.

Shaking his head as she disappeared out the end of the stable, he finished tacking up his horse, unhooking the lead rope, and swinging into the saddle.

Adjusting the reins and urging his horse forward, he hit the end of the stable just as Carna motored along with the four-wheeler.

She'd figured out there were circles cut in the back of the ATV that were perfect to set a bucket in.

It had taken him a couple of times holding a bucket in his lap before he realized the four-wheeler was equipped to carry them.

He was kind of impressed that she figured it out right away.

"If you follow this road, you'll come to the sign you saw when you first came in. Just take the other branch, and I'll meet you over there, okay? I'm going to go through the field, rounding up the horses as I do that. Pushing them over. Typically once they see someone there with the grain, they'll go right to the trough, and we'll have our pick of them. They have to head through a gate, and I can close it behind them, and we'll have them when we're ready for them."

"How many are there?"

"There are nine horses in the field. And Smith texted me and said four people in the group."

"Good to know."

"I'll meet you over there," he said, and she nodded, starting the four-wheeler and motoring away.

He walked through the yard, knowing there wasn't a huge rush and not wanting to get his horse all lathered up, nor did he want to scare the horses that were in the field.

Sherlock was a well-trained horse, and he did a nice side pass so Miller didn't have to dismount to open the gate.

The horses were in a group about halfway through, and he just carefully pushed them over to the other side at a walk.

They naturally moved away from him, and just like he'd asked, Carna was on the other side with the bucket, shaking it and pouring it into the trough as soon as they noticed her.

After that, they went right to the gate, filed in, and he shut it behind them.

Moseying over to the fence to watch the horses eat, he casually said, "These horses are all beginner safe. Do you see one that you'd like to try?"

"Any of them?" she asked.

"Sure. These are all picked so that someone who has zero horse experience can still use them to trail ride."

"I see. Do you have any recommendations for me?"

"Are you scared or eager?" he asked.

"Both?"

He laughed. "All right, then I don't think that one is any better than the others, but one of my favorites is Dolly. She's the little palomino over at the end. She's pretty low on the totem pole—the herd has a pecking order—but she's a sweetheart, and she'll be in your pocket the whole time."

"Palomino. That means a brown body and a cream-colored tail and mane?"

"Yeah."

"I see her. She's pretty."

"Palominos are probably my favorite coloring, although you can get some paints that are pretty flashy, and they'll catch the eye."

"Like that one?" She pointed to a pretty paint on the end.

"So you know a little bit about horses."

"I've read books about horses, but that's all I know. It's a lot different when you try to put book knowledge and head knowledge into actual experience. Sometimes things don't work out quite the way you picture them, and things go sideways."

"That's happened to me a time or two. I wish we could give you at least a short ride before we go out on the trail, but there's just no time. If that dust cloud is any indication, our guests are on their way. Would you like to walk in and grab your horse?"

"Sure."

He pointed to the covered rack where they had the halters and leads. "Grab one of those. I'll give you a hand, but she's easy to catch. They all are once they're in here."

By the time they caught Dolly, led her out of the field, and tied her to a hitching post, the car had stopped at the office.

One of the ladies had gone in, while the other three got out of the car. All women.

Miller was particularly grateful that Carna would be along. It wasn't that women scared him exactly, but he wasn't great at knowing what to talk to them about.

Sometimes people wanted to take a trail ride and just talk amongst the group, and at other times, they wanted him to talk with them or to them. To them wasn't hard, because they would ask questions about the ranch and want to know the history or the history of the area or things to see and do. That was easy. He'd kind of gotten his spiel down pat, but when they wanted him to talk with them, small talk type things, more personal things, then it got a little harder.

Carna would hopefully ease some of the pressure there for him.

His phone buzzed in his pocket, and he pulled it out to read the text that Darby, working in the office, sent him.

Four ladies, an afternoon trail ride and picnic. They're checked in and going over the safety instructions. As soon as they sign

the waivers, they'll be heading out.

A second text came.

Stop at the kitchen; the picnic's ready.

Carna's phone had buzzed the same time his did, and he saw that she was in on the group text.

He lifted his eyes, brows up, and said, "You ready?"

"This is what we do. I guess I have to be ready."

She didn't seem overly anxious, although she didn't seem excited either. Like she had a job to do, and she was going to do it.

For him, he actually was kind of looking forward to it. She'd turned out to be a pretty good partner to work with. He liked working with people who pulled their weight, who didn't complain and didn't have a bunch of dramatics.

She could have made things really difficult over the fact that she had no clue on how to ride a horse.

Thankfully, she hadn't.

"Before they come out, let me give you a couple of pointers that will make riding a horse easier. For the most part, Dolly is a point her where you want and she'll go kind of horse. I'll put you in the back, and she'll follow the group. All you have to do is stop her when we stop. And actually, she'll probably do that on her own too. Have you ever watched anyone get up?

Left foot in the stirrup, then swing your right foot over."

He spoke low, keeping an eye on the office door to make sure that he got all the instructions in before anyone came out. It wasn't his goal to embarrass her but to make it so that she didn't seem like a total greenhorn. If she wanted to admit that she'd never ridden a horse before, he was fine with it, but he didn't want to totally leave her in the dark.

"Is it going to embarrass you if I tell everyone this is my first time on a horse?" she asked as he stopped to think about whether there was anything else he needed to say.

"No. Totally up to you. I just wanted to give you some personal instructions, because when they come out, our attention is going to have to be on them. I'm probably not going to be able to help you the way I would like to."

He could have kicked himself for saying that. He didn't really mean that he wanted to help her. Except...he did. He didn't want to see her struggle. Didn't want to see her not do it as well as she wanted to.

Then, her lips kicked up a little, and she didn't tease him about it. She just said, "Thanks, Ducky Doo Doo."

He snorted. "Anytime, Tater Tot."

They grinned at each other, and he got the idea that maybe she wasn't annoyed about her nickname, any more than he was annoyed about his. Could that be true?

Maybe. Probably.

It didn't take long after that for the ladies to check in at the office. Miller had barely gotten Carna's horse tacked up when they came walking over.

He dusted his hands off on his pants and started walking beside Carna to meet them.

Chapter 15

Carna sucked in a breath. The time of reckoning. She knew when she came out here that this was what they did, she just didn't think she would be doing it. There were so many other people on the ranch, she thought for sure she'd get stuck somewhere mucking out stalls and fixing fence. Which she wouldn't mind at all. She knew how to do those things at least.

This...this was a whole different ball game.

And she had to say, she really appreciated Miller taking her aside just now and telling her what she needed to do, giving her a little encouragement, half pep talk, half instruction.

It eased her mind so much more than what she could say.

It was almost like he was being...nice.

Which shouldn't surprise her. Miller always had been a nice guy, except with her. Actually, he had never been mean to her, other than the last twenty-four hours, but had always just teased her mercilessly.

Of course she'd given it right back, so she couldn't complain.

She walked beside Miller as they took a couple of steps to meet the ladies who were walking toward them.

Miller held out his hand to the first lady, the tallest in the group. "I'm Miller, this is Carna. We're going to be your guides today."

"I'm Danielle. And we're really excited to be on an actual ranch." She shook his hand, enthusiastically giving him a wide smile.

Carna wanted to clear her throat, since Danielle had apparently forgotten that he'd introduced her too.

She stepped forward, holding out her hand, and said, "I'm Carna," even though she'd already been introduced.

Danielle's hand lingered a bit in Miller's, and she gave him a wink, before she pulled her perfectly manicured nails, that glinted pink in the sunlight, away from Miller.

"Carna. Interesting name." That was all she said, although her bracelets jangled as she pumped Carna's hand.

Her earrings shifted in the sunlight, pretty unicorns that dangled an inch below her lobes.

Her hair lay in waves around her shoulders, and her designer jeans fit her like a second skin.

Her T-shirt emphasized all of her curves. And it was rather low-cut for a T-shirt.

"Did you bring sunscreen? You might need it, considering that we're going to be out in the sun the rest of the afternoon," Carna said, thinking that she probably should have thought about that for herself.

Her arms were already browned, but she liked to at least protect her face.

"We already put suntan lotion on," Danielle said, dismissing Carna and turning back to Miller. "These are my girlfriends, Robin, Jan, and Kathy." She pointed to each woman as she said their name.

Miller gave a tight smile and shook each of their hands. The other ladies smiled at Carna and shook her hand as well.

"I'll be in charge, and Carna is my assistant. If you need anything, just ask one of us, and we'll figure things out." He turned to Carna, and she read a question in his eyes. She figured, if she was going to admit that this was her first ride, this was the time for her to do it.

She didn't want to pretend that she was anything other than what she was, so she said, "Miller could have added that this is my first ride. I've never ridden a horse before in my life, although I've worked on farms for the last decade or more. So animals in general are not new to me, and farmwork is second nature."

She didn't want them to think she wasn't knowledgeable. They were paying for the whole ranch experience, not for a greenhorn to lead them around. They could do that for themselves.

"She has a natural affinity with animals that I think you can see if you watch her with her dog," Miller said as he nodded to Posey who was lying down with her head on her paws not far from Carna's feet.

She was surprised he had noticed anything about her and Posey and even more surprised that he would mention it. Maybe he too was trying to convince the ladies that they weren't wasting their money.

"We've all taken riding lessons. That was part of our education at the private school we attended on Long Island," Danielle said with a bit of snobbery in her voice, like meeting someone who had never ridden a horse was somewhat beneath her, but she was going to put up with it just this once.

"You look like you've grown up on a horse," she said, casting an admiring look at Miller.

Miller looked a little bit uncomfortable and ignored her, other than jerking his head to acknowledge her statement. "The horses you can choose from are behind us in the field. If you see one that catches your eye, let us know, and we'll snag it for you and saddle it up."

"You mean we can choose any one of them?" the shortest girl said. She was dressed very similarly to Danielle, in designer jeans and brand-new cowgirl boots, with perfectly manicured nails and a somewhat less low-cut T-shirt.

She seemed sweet and kind, and Carna really liked her.

"Sure. Any of them should be good for any level of rider." Miller's words were casual as he turned to lean on the fence, looking at the herd that had finished up all the grain that was in the trough and now milled about.

"I want that dun. Man, he's pretty. Although he's a little smaller than what I'm used to. We mostly rode English in school." There was a lot of snobbery in Danielle's voice, and Carna got the feeling that she considered Western to be the lesser of the two disciplines.

Considering that Carna had never ridden English or Western, she really couldn't say, but she figured it just depended on what a person wanted to do.

"I can grab him," Carna said, taking a look at the horse to make sure it actually was a gelding.

"That's a good choice. Badger is a great horse." Miller nodded approvingly, and Danielle beamed.

Carna walked away from them, grabbing a halter and lead from the covered rack, then opening the gate and walking inside.

Thankfully, Badger let her walk right up to him, and by the time she led him back, Miller had gone after a different horse.

She took them over to the hitching post where Miller had tied Dolly, then she turned back to the ladies. "Does someone else have a horse that they would like?"

"I like the black one. It has the four socks, and those are really pretty," one of the girls said, smiling sweetly. Carna was pretty sure that was Jan, and she nodded her head. "I'll bring her right back," she said, realizing it was a little mare.

She really was pretty with her black coat and flashy socks.

She grabbed her and got the halter on, when Miller came by, leading the horse that he had, which had been slightly harder to catch, walking away from him when he walked toward it.

"I'll grab these two, if you find out what the last lady wants."

Carna thanked him, because she had no idea how to start tacking up the horses. She had so much to learn.

She had thought being on a farm would be pretty straightforward, but every minute she spent here made her feel like she wasn't the slightest bit prepared.

Robin, the last woman, picked out her horse, and thankfully Carna got that one with no problem as well.

Miller acted like he'd done it a time or two, which he probably had, and he had all of them helping a little bit with their horses, brushing off their backs, making sure the hair was all laid down the way it was supposed to, and showing them how to tack up.

Danielle flirted, almost outrageously, with him, but he didn't seem to notice, although he was kind back to her.

It annoyed Carna a little, but she supposed it shouldn't. It was probably good for business. If the ladies were here to see an actual "cowboy," flirting was probably what they wanted.

They were probably disappointed that his assistant was a woman.

Thankfully, they finished saddling the horses up, and Carna didn't make too much of a fool out of herself, helping where she could and hanging on Miller's every word.

"I think you're going to need to tighten your cinch on Dolly. I saddled her, but sometimes she holds her breath a bit, and you need to tighten it after she's not thinking about it anymore."

"Oh. Thank you."

He went through the line while she was doing that, and made sure that every-one had tightened their cinches nice and tight, checking the tack to make sure it was all on the way it was supposed to be.

"If you need a mounting block, there is one right over there. If you think you can get on here on the ground, you're wel-come to mount up. Carna, if you don't mind running over to the kitchen and grabbing the picnic supplies that they have for us, I'll grab one last horse, and we'll put the packs on him."

Carna jerked her head and strode to-ward the kitchen.

By the time she came back with two baskets and a blanket, Miller had one last horse out of pasture, and while he didn't have a saddle on him, he had some kind of odd-looking contraption where the baskets were able to fit on either side, and the blanket lay over the middle.

It was a neat way to carry things and something she'd never seen before.

The other ladies led their horses over to the mounting block.

Miller turned toward her and asked, "Do you need a hand?"

"No. I think I can do it." She had no such confidence, but she didn't want to have special treatment, especially since she was supposed to be leading and not following.

"If you don't mind, I'll keep a hand on Dolly, just to make sure you do it. Not because I don't think you can, but because it's your first time. I just want to help," he said low, like he truly didn't want her to try to mount and fall on her butt.

She trusted him, at least believed that for the sake of the ranch he wasn't going to do anything unkind, and she nodded her head, giving him a small smile.

As she walked over to her horse, he led the packhorse behind her, and as far as she could tell, he acted casually, like he wasn't doing anything special for her, just waiting for her to mount so he could tie the packhorse to her saddle horn.

Thankfully, she got up without any problems, although she had to admit having him stand behind her, knowing that he would catch her if she needed it, gave her confidence that she hadn't realized she lacked.

"Good job," he said softly so the other ladies couldn't hear. A little louder he said, "I'm going to tie Comet to your saddle horn, which is the way we usually do it. Whoever's in the back leads the packhorse." He lowered his voice. "He's the horse that hardly anyone ever chooses. I'm not sure what it is about him. Maybe just because he's a dull brown color. I don't know. But he's a great horse, and he won't give you any trouble."

She appreciated him saying that, because she was a little bit concerned. Here she was, riding a horse for the first time, and now not only was she going to be riding for the first time, but she would be leading one, too.

"Thanks for helping me. I do appreciate it," she said, and there was no trace of the earlier antagonism in her voice.

She really appreciated him being the first to apologize and being willing to hold out an olive branch earlier the way he had with the color of shirts they were going to wear.

It had made the day so much easier for her. She needed to remember to thank him.

Chapter 16

It had been a nice three and a half hours. Much better than he thought it could be. Now, they were just thirty minutes away from the ranch, and Miller was grateful that Carna seemed to be completely at ease.

She wasn't exactly a born horse-woman, but she'd done well on her horse, had sucked it up if she had been scared to the point where he hadn't even noticed, and had been sweet and funny with the ladies.

Danielle seemed to only want to talk to him, and she followed directly beside him.

She'd asked several personal questions, which he brushed off, and the rest of the ladies had gotten the hint.

They'd talked about attractions in the area, what the ladies did in New York City, how long they'd known each other, and Carna and he had even admitted that they grew up together.

"I think I read on the brochure that you used to be in the Air Force?" Danielle said, and Miller managed to keep from groaning. It wasn't that he didn't want to talk about the Air Force, he was just ready to be home. Ready to unsaddle the horses and be away from people for a while.

The ladies had been a great group, but he wasn't quite done with his job, so he took a breath and said, "I was. A bunch of us were."

"That's what it said on the brochure. I always admire a man in uniform. Thank you so much for your service," Danielle said, and she sounded thankful, sure, but she also sounded flirty as well.

"I enjoyed it. I've always loved flying."

"Oh my goodness, you fly?"

"It's the Air Force, you doofus," one of the other ladies over to the side said.

He wondered if Carna could hear them, since she was riding behind and to the side.

He supposed she probably couldn't, with his voice projecting forward, and a couple ladies had their own private conversation going on.

"Not everybody in the Air Force flies planes. There are a lot of other jobs, including mechanics, air support, tech support, and on and on. But the reason I joined was because I loved flying, so while I didn't fly much in the Air Force, I did get my private pilot's license, and we do some crop dusting and that type of thing."

"Oh my goodness, you still fly?"

Danielle sounded way more impressed than what that entailed, and he just said, "Yep."

"Oh my goodness. It's so dangerous."

"It's really not."

"Have you ever had any near miss-es?" one of the other ladies asked. He thought it might have been Jan, but he wasn't sure. He hadn't talked to them enough to be able to pin a voice with a name without seeing her face.

"Once, when I first got my license, I was goofing off in the airplane. Most of the smaller airplanes that you used to get your license are pretty maneuver-able in the air, and I wasn't exactly do-ing a loop or anything, but I was pulling out of a shallow dive, and I guess I had enough Gs that it made me pass out. I couldn't have been out long, but I was out long enough to scare me. I...didn't do too much messing around in the air after that. Typically, when you're driving a car, you don't get to the point where you make yourself pass out."

"Oh my goodness. And you didn't wreck?"

"I was only out for a second or two. I mean, when you've blacked out, you don't know how much time is passing, but I know I was climbing when I passed out, and I hadn't quite leveled off when I woke up. But I was slumped over the controls, and they were pushing a little downward, so if I hadn't woken up, I probably would have done a nosedive into the ground."

The ladies behind him gasped, and he wondered if he should even have told that story.

Hopefully Carna didn't hear it, although maybe she didn't care enough about him that it would bother her if anything happened to him.

The wind gusted, and he was grateful that the ranch had come into sight. Another ten minutes, and they would have made it home before the rain.

All in all, it hadn't been a terrible day, and he had to admit that that was at least partially due to the fact that just the idea that Carna was along had made the trip a lot more fun.

Chapter 17

Carna dismounted, for the second time in her life, and she managed to land on her feet. She'd done it earlier too and had been grateful that she hadn't landed on her butt, since her legs had been more unresponsive than she expected.

She ached in places she didn't know a person could ache and figured she'd know it and be sore in a lot more places in the morning.

Not that she cared. She was grateful that she was able to go and, if not pull her weight, at least be a body that enabled them to have a trail ride, since Miller had told her that Smith insisted two employees go on every ride.

She figured that was probably for legal purposes, but she didn't ask.

Regardless, they needed to get the horses unsaddled, and soon, and get inside, or they were going to get wet.

"It's been a pleasure, ladies. I'm so glad you chose to ride with us today," Carna said in what she hoped wasn't a promotional-sounding voice. She would get used to this, but it was odd to have someone who was a complete stranger yesterday be someone she enjoyed and wouldn't mind being friends with today, but to also know that she would most likely never see them again.

"Thanks so much for sharing your expertise with us," Danielle said, batting her eyes at Miller like she'd been doing for the last four hours.

It annoyed Carna, but it annoyed her even more when he smiled back at her.

That was the polite thing to do, and Carna couldn't fault him. Not really. Plus, Miller seemed to enjoy the attention.

Of course he did. What person wouldn't? Danielle was beautiful and successful, and anyone would enjoy being around her.

Carna would enjoy being around her much more if she weren't flirting so heavily with Miller.

Regardless, it wasn't any of her business who Miller flirted with, or who he didn't, so she turned back and chatted with Robin and Jan, who were just as sweet as they could be.

Kathy had seemed to have fallen in love with her horse and didn't want to let her go. She was standing in front of her, with both hands on either cheek, her forehead resting against her forehead, as she whispered in a sad voice to her.

Ignoring Danielle who was chattering to Miller behind her, she walked over and took the reins of Robin's and Jan's horses. "Thanks so much for coming, I hope you come back."

"It was so much fun. It was just completely relaxing and amazing to go so far and not see a single building or house. Just wide-open sky." Jan's eyes shone, and there was no doubt that she was happy with her experience. Carna was grateful that at least someone other than her had a great time.

"I almost wish we would have gotten caught in the rain. That would have been fun." Robin laughed, shrugging her shoulders apologetically. "I'm sure that none of you would have liked to get wet, but I just love storms, and it would have been an experience to talk about. Not that this wasn't already fabulous. And give my compliments to the cook. The potato salad was the best I've ever had."

"I'll be sure to tell her. I know she'll appreciate it."

The three of them walked off, and Carna turned back to Miller, unsure what to do with the horses. She'd watched him saddle them all up and thought that she might be able to do that by herself, but she hadn't seen a single horse be un-saddled and wasn't sure where to start, other than just starting at the end and going backward. But she didn't want to mess anything up, so she figured she'd ask.

"Oh my goodness. They're leaving already." Danielle glanced after her friends, then put a hand on Miller's fore-arm, and said, "I'll be in town. Maybe we can meet up later?"

"I'll be working until dark." Miller shrugged, like there wasn't anything he could do about it, but it also served to move his arm so her hand dropped from it.

"I'm sorry to interrupt, but I'm not sure exactly where to start here, and I need a little instruction. If you don't mind?"

Miller didn't look relieved, but he didn't look annoyed that she'd interrupted them either. If he wanted to spend more time with Danielle, she'd issued an open invitation for this evening, and he basically turned her down. Maybe he was going to suggest they do something after dark, but he could do it after he was done showing her what to do so she could get on with her work.

"Maybe after you're done working, you'll come in?" Danielle said with a dismissive glance at Carna, angling her shoulder so it was obvious that she wanted to keep the conversation between Miller and herself.

"No, thank you," Miller said simply.

"Well, if you change your mind," Danielle said, holding up a slip of paper between her first and second fingers before she tucked it into Miller's front pocket.

He didn't cringe back when she touched him, and Carna turned away, deciding that she would grab the cinch and see if she could loosen it herself.

She figured she'd start on Dolly, who had been a total angel the entire time, but the leather was tight, and she wasn't exactly sure how to loosen it.

She tried to get her hands in between the leather and the horse's hide, and she could do that, but she couldn't move the strap in either direction.

"Do it like this," Miller said, coming around and taking hold of the leather, lifting up with one hand, and pushing up on the end with the other.

She could see how that would loosen the tension on the knot and make it easier to pull out.

"I should have thought of that," she said.

"I don't know why you would have if you've never seen it done before."

"Well, I haven't, but I have now. Is there anything else I need to know?" she asked as she stepped forward, ready to take over.

He paused but didn't let go of the cinch. "No. But I did want to thank you. You did a great job. Especially considering it was your first time. If you were scared or unsure, I couldn't tell."

"I was both, but I'm glad to hear that I did okay."

"You did more than okay. Thank you."

She jerked her head, then stepped back toward her horse, causing him to step back, while she took over loosening the cinch and letting it fall to the ground.

"If you get the saddles off, I'll carry them over to the shed. The rain's going to be starting, and I'd like to get them in so they don't get wet."

"All right." She set the saddle on the saddle stand while he took a second one off.

She worked as fast as she could, doing it the way he showed her, but her fingers weren't accustomed to the work, and as a beginner, she did a lot of fumbling. It was a struggle not to get frustrated, especially when the horse she worked on moved under her.

It ended up that Miller got everything else done, while she barely managed to get five saddles off.

Still, she knew she'd get faster, and she tried not to be down on herself because it was her first time.

"Are you mad at me?" he asked as he stood at her elbow, waiting for her to pull the last saddle off. She hadn't quite figured out how to get it off without pulling the pad and having it fall on the ground other than holding onto the pad with her fingers, and that was what she was concentrating on doing. However, at his words, she stopped.

"Mad?" she asked, wrinkling up her nose.

"You haven't said hardly anything since the guests left."

The car had gone out not long after Danielle had said goodbye to him, and Carna had tried not to give them another thought.

"No. I'm not mad."

"I just wondered. I thought we kind of developed a truce, but now you're not talking."

"I'm sorry," she said, not elaborating. He was right. She hadn't been talking, and she could probably blame it on concentrating on what she was doing, but that wasn't really true. "I'm not mad at you."

"It just seems like you are." He didn't say anything else, just stood with the rope around the horse's neck, waiting for her to pull the saddle off so he could rub her down and let her out.

"I guess I thought maybe you wanted to go out with Danielle, and maybe you said no because I was standing there. It was just one more time today where I felt like I was in the way."

That wasn't exactly it either, but she honestly couldn't put her finger on what her problem really was. She didn't like him flirting with Danielle, but he wasn't being any friendlier than what she was. He wanted them to come back, after all. To go home to their friends and tell them they'd had a great time here. So of course he wanted to be friendly and to make sure they enjoyed themselves.

"I didn't want to."

Well, that was helpful. But it didn't really make her feel better. "I just thought I was maybe crowding in. But I want to get this done before it rains, and I'm concentrating."

As she spoke, the wind gusted again, feeling cool and bringing the scent of petrichor with a few drops of cool water with it.

She breathed deeply, loving that smell.

She couldn't help but notice that he did too.

She might have smiled at him, but she wasn't feeling...like they were a team anymore? She wasn't sure exactly what it was. She just felt like Danielle was between them, and while that didn't bother her exactly, it made her feel like she didn't want to be close to someone who preferred to be close to someone else. That was the best she could do to explain it.

"I think we're just barely going to make it," he said as he brushed the horse's back with broad strokes of the brush, then led her to the pasture, while Carna grabbed the saddle, pulled the cinch up so it didn't drag on the ground, and hurried to the shed where he put the other ones.

There was one last saddle rack that was empty, and she threw the saddle on it, putting the saddle pad upside down overtop of it as he'd done with the others.

A flash of lightning split the sky, and thunder rumbled as she turned back toward the opening of the shed.

Miller jogged the last twenty yards as the rain let loose and flooded the yard, almost instantly.

"Wow. Like a dam broke," Miller said as he ducked inside, shaking his arms off and pulling his shirt away from his chest.

It wasn't soaked, but he definitely got wet.

"I'd say perfect timing, but maybe we could have been about ten seconds earlier."

She nodded, watching the rain as it fell and thinking that rain in North Dakota looked the same as rain anywhere else she'd ever been. Some things were vastly different, and some things were achingly familiar.

She remembered standing at the edge of the milk stable, in the doorway where the cows went out into the barnyard. There was a step down, and she would stand at the edge while waiting for a cow to finish milking so she could change the milker, watching the storms roll in, watching fat drops of rain come down, feeling safe and snug inside the stable with the warm breath of the cows and the familiar hum of the milk pump, and the rhythmic beat of the air pressure and release.

That ache, the one that felt physical and deep, pulled at her soul again. She supposed it was homesickness.

"You gonna tell me what I did?" Miller asked her once again.

She blinked, surprised to feel her eyes prick as she pulled her mind back to the present. "No. You didn't do anything. I... I guess I'm just tired."

"I don't believe that. I kinda liked us getting along, and I was hoping that that was going to be a permanent thing."

"I hope it will be too. I want it to be."

"All right. I'll quit asking. But if you want to tell me what exactly I did, I'll be listening." He turned away from her, leaning his shoulder against the side of the doorjamb, and looked out at the rain.

"I told you it wasn't about you." She had to talk loud to be heard over the pounding rain on the roof of the shed.

The horses were soaked, but they didn't seem to be bothered by the rain.

They just had their tails to the wind, their heads down.

Miller didn't say anything, but she got the feeling that he was annoyed with her. More than he'd been with her all afternoon when she really had been a liability. It made her feel like he seriously wanted to get along with her and it bothered him that there was something between them. But what could she say when she didn't even know what bothered her?

"I guess... I guess I just kinda feel like I was somehow in the way between you and Danielle. And not in a romantic sense or anything, just...like things might have been a little different between the two of you if I hadn't been there."

That wasn't a very good way to explain it, but she wasn't jealous. She wasn't angry. She just...wanted to be away from him, because it felt like he wanted someone else. She hated that he was stuck with her, and she didn't want to be the reason that he couldn't go if he wanted to.

"And I told you that I was happy she left and I didn't want to go with her. Are you jealous?" He looked over at her, and the expression on his face showed that he didn't really believe it but didn't know what else to think.

"No. I'm not. You guys just seemed to have a good time together, and I felt a little awkward. A little intrusive. A little bit like...I just wanted to get away."

"You can stop feeling like that, because it's not true. Danielle was way too high maintenance for me. And there was no point in spending any time with her, because we're never going to be anything more than whatever kind of fling she wanted to have while she was out here. I'm not into flings."

Chapter 18

Carna nodded her head, appreciating Miller's explanation but still not quite feeling happy. Maybe it was the idea that she would never be what Danielle was. Beautiful, put together, perfectly manicured, and totally confident. Confident enough to grab a man by the arm and invite him to...do something with her later. She wasn't like that and didn't want to be like that, but she admired that confidence. Maybe it was the obvious difference between Danielle's confidence and her own ineptitude and the idea that Danielle had been a better match to work with Miller than she was.

"She had a lot of confidence. I admire that," Carna said instead.

"Confidence is attractive to anyone," Miller agreed, his eyes still on the rain.

"That's true," Carna said, pushing aside the nostalgic thoughts and the longing for happier days when her grandparents were still on the farm and she helped them. When things seemed a lot simpler, but maybe that was just because she didn't have the bills to pay. She had a lot of good memories of those times, and she supposed someday she should be able to get them out without them making her feel sad. The idea that there was no escape, that this was the place where she had to be, whether she liked it or not, whether Miller was with Danielle and she felt like a third wheel or not didn't matter.

"You know you're confident." Miller's words were low, and she barely heard them over the rain.

"So are you. You just start walking and assume that everybody's gonna follow you." She had laughed at that a little bit, although a couple of times, it felt like he'd slowed his steps so she could catch up. Certainly his dog went wherever he did.

Currently both dogs were lying down with their heads on their paws, sleeping through the rainstorm.

She looked down, smiling. "That's a good thing to do when it rains. Take a nap."

"Sometimes I think that dogs are a lot smarter than people," Miller said, lifting his brows at her and smiling a little.

"I don't know that I've ever thought that before, but I have to agree. Certainly they brush things off a lot easier than we do and don't hold grudges."

"They don't typically get stubborn either. I do that."

"I hadn't noticed," she said ironically.

"Hey. I'm the one who gave in about the shirt. You're the one who was stubborn."

"I guess you're right about that. I do have a tendency to be stubborn, and I know it. I wish I could fix it just by wanting not to be, you know? That doesn't happen, though. Just because you want to do something, you want to be kind, you want to be outgoing. You want to be patient. It doesn't just happen. You have to...make a conscious effort to realize that you're going to do or be something that you really don't want to do or be, and then you have to deliberately choose to do something else."

"That's true, but the good part about that is, the more you do it, the easier it becomes, until you don't have to have that deliberate thought in your head any longer. You don't have to make a conscious effort, it becomes something that's natural."

"Well, it seems to take me a lot longer than normal people to get to that point."

"I doubt it. Some people are just better at realizing that they need to take those thoughts and turn them around. Of course, it helps if you think beforehand that the next time you get upset, you're going to get a hold of yourself, and you're going to ask yourself some questions that will help you realize that your answers are showing you you don't want to do what you're doing."

"That was vague."

He laughed. "All right. Say every time I go on a trail ride, there's some woman who goes along with me, who grabs hold of me, flirts with me, and makes me uncomfortable. I want to turn around and walk away and leave her in the field for the buzzards. I have to say to myself, I'm going to be nice to this person, no matter how flirty and clingy she is, because that's the best thing for the ranch."

"I bet you really had to talk yourself into being nice." She rolled her eyes.

"All right. I admit, I didn't think that at all. Although, those are my least favorite kind of people to lead around. The other three girls were pretty nice, but you could have taken Danielle and hung out with her all day and it wouldn't have bothered me at all."

"A different example?" she prodded, not wanting to go back to the subject of Danielle. There was too much there that bothered her.

"All right."

He pretended to think a minute, but she kinda thought that he was just messing with her, making it more dramatic than what it needed to be.

"Say I'm in the field and I'm working with the horses. I know I need to be more patient when I'm trying to teach the foal to lead, but it's just so aggravating when they don't get it. And I've gone over it and over it and over it."

He grinned a little. "Kind of like a parent with their kids, only probably that happens on a daily basis, and you can't exactly choose when it's going to happen. So it's probably harder. But anyway, with the foal, I can think to myself, do I want to be impatient with this foal? Of course not. It's going to be worth a lot of money someday, and I'm going to want to make sure that it's trained correctly. I don't want it to be afraid of humans, and therefore I don't want to lose my temper with it. If I do, I could end up messing up where I actually give myself more work to do, because then I have to teach it to trust me again before I can continue with whatever it was that I was trying to teach it in the first place. So, I know for a fact that if I get irritated, I just need to stop what I'm doing and walk away. It's not going to hurt anything, and I'm not going to gain anything by pushing through and forcing the foal to do what I want it to do. Does that make sense?"

"All right. That's a pretty good example. And I think you're right, you could probably apply that to children or even to other people," she said with a laugh. "For example, people that you work with. I don't know, say someone you're going on a trail ride with, and they're irritating you."

"This feels really familiar." He gave her a side glance. "Do you by chance have anyone in particular in mind?"

"No. Purely hypothetical." She pursed her lips but didn't meet his eyes. "You can think to yourself, I want the ranch to be successful. I want to be a good example for the ranch. I want to bring in customers, not drive people away. If I am impatient or unkind, they will almost assuredly give me a bad review, and then where am I going to be? Not to mention, on top of that, everything that I do should point people to Jesus. Do I want those people to look at me and say 'if that's the way a Christian acts, I certainly don't want to be one,' and walk away?"

"And there you go. The biggest reason to be patient and kind and considerate. Because it's not just about the ranch making money, although there are a lot of people who depend on us for that, but as you pointed out, we drive people away from the Lord when they know we're Christians, and we don't act like it."

They grinned at each other, but there was a seriousness behind their expressions that made Carna reevaluate her assessment, yet again, of Miller. He wasn't the teenager she knew. That, she'd already figured out, but he'd grown and matured in ways that hadn't been obvious at first.

In fact, she had to admit, he actually impressed her.

She turned away first, looking at the rain which had slackened off a little to a steady downpour. Not the deluge of earlier.

He turned to her, and one of the dogs whined behind them, but neither one of them got up.

"How did you end up with Pepper? Has he been yours from a puppy?"

"Kind of," Miller said easily, shifting a little so that his shoulder was still leaning against the doorframe but it was easier for him to look over at her. "Someone dropped him off on the driveway. I didn't really take him in, he just was something else we fed. Lark came and gave him his rabies shot, and eventually we had her give him some other shots and fix him. She doesn't typically Doo Doogs, but she did it for us since we're one of her big customers."

"Lark's a vet?"

"She and Mabel are the best around here. They practice together, and if you don't get one, you'll get the other."

"I see," she murmured, wondering how old Lark was, and if she were married.

Miller didn't seem to be interested in her in that way, at least his expression didn't change while he was talking about her, which made her even more curious.

About Lark, but also about Miller.

"So, once he got familiar with the place and everything, I'm not sure why he picked me, but he started following me around. I never took him up with me when I went into my apartment at night, and he was probably less than a year old when we got him. He looked young, but I don't think he grew much since he came, so maybe he wasn't as young as what I thought. Anyway, I was the one he latched onto. And that's really the end of the story."

"You've worked with him a little?" Carna probed just a little deeper. He acted like it wasn't a big deal, but it was pretty obvious that he loved the dog.

"Oh sure. It's North Dakota, I need something to do in the winter. I worked with him on different commands, and he's a decent cattle dog. He might have a little bit of that kind of blood running through his veins, but it's not something he'll ever excel at. We wouldn't win any competitions, but he gives us a hand when we need it, and that seems to be enough to make him happy."

She nodded, looking at the dog with a little bit of a smile. He was a good dog. Although she would never trade him for Posey.

"What about yours? I assume she's been yours since she was young?"

"Actually no. She was my grandparents' dog. They got her a couple years after I started working for them. The neighbor's dog had puppies, and they were giving them away. They took one, and she's been theirs ever since."

"But she's here now."

"I mean, yeah. Right. They...had to go to a nursing home...in the case of my grandfather, the last few months. For my grandmother, I took care of her at home until the last few weeks or so. It was just too much trying to work on the farm and take care of her, and there was so much... I... I wanted to keep it going, but the bills were too high, and they had to sell it to pay for the nursing care for Pap. I think that probably made Gram go a little faster. She loved the farm, almost as much as she loved Pap, and losing them both... It was just too much."

"They took the farm to pay for their care?"

"Yeah. They'll take your assets and sell them in order to pay for whatever care you get, that comes first before any state aid. It's... It's not really fair, but that's the way life is, I guess. Some people get around it by deeding their farm to their kids or grandkids or whatever, years be-fore they need to move to a facility. The problem with that is, once it's not in your name anymore, the people who own it can do whatever they want to."

"Like? Make decisions you don't agree with?"

"Sure. Or sell it out from underneath you. Then you have no choice but to move out. If your name's not on it anymore, it's not yours. I've actually seen several cases where that's happened. Sad as it is."

"I believe it. People will do pretty much anything for money. Even sell out their grandparents, I guess."

"Yeah. You like to think that that would never happen, but it does."

They were quiet for a bit as the rain tapered off to a steady drizzle, the wind dying down, and the lightning and thunder moving out.

"I don't usually get to watch the rain from this vantage point. This was nice," Miller said eventually, breaking the silence that had fallen between them.

It had been a comfortable silence, one she hadn't felt the need to fill. Or felt uncomfortable in. There weren't a whole lot of people who could stand around in an easy silence, and she appreciated the fact that Miller was one of those people.

"What are you gonna do for supper?" Miller asked, and it seemed like a casual question.

"I don't know. Yesterday, you brought leftovers from lunch home for supper, and that was a good idea. Unfortunately, there wasn't too much left from lunch."

"No. There wasn't..." He shifted. "How do you feel about going to the diner for supper?"

Don't overthink this.

It was just a matter of both of them needing to eat and him suggesting the reasonable thing. After all, she knew as well as he did that there were no groceries or food of any kind in the apartment.

"I know we can go to the house, and they'll feed us. Anyone's always welcome at the table. I just... After a day's work, it's nice for them to be able to spend a little time with just their family, especially when they have a job like we do, where you have people coming in and out all the time and never really any privacy or family time. It's going to get even worse this summer before it gets better. Anyway, that's what I'm going to do, and... If you want to join me, I...would be okay with it."

"All right. When you put it like that, or I guess you didn't need to put it any certain way. I thought of the empty cupboards, and I knew I needed to do something. But I'm with you. I know we're welcome anytime, but I hate to impose on their family time."

"All right. I don't always get cleaned up before I go into town, but I think I might today. After all, I'm still a little bit wet, and I smell an awful lot like horse."

"If I don't get cleaned up, I'm going to make people lose their appetite, and I wouldn't want to do that, so I'd better take a shower too."

"All right." He paused. "I put Sherlock in with the other horses. I'm going to grab him to take him back to the stable on my way back over. So, I'll catch you on the other side, okay?"

She grinned, nodding, and watched as he walked away.

His stride, confident and easy, drew her eye.

But it was his principles, his outlook on life. His thoughts about how he wanted-ed to deliberately make decisions about how he acted and not just respond to the stimuli around him that she felt drawn to.

It was hard to believe that this was the teenager that she felt antagonistic toward all her life. He'd grown into an interesting and complicated and...attractive man.

Chapter 19

Travis stood at the edge of the room, trying to remember not to pull at the collar of his starched white shirt. His tie was way too tight. It felt like it was choking him, but that's the way it always felt when he wore one.

Growing up, he hadn't even owned a tie. Not until he had gone to Chicago for Ford Hansen.

This was not the first black tie event Ford had had him attend, but it was the largest. Also the most formal and fancy.

They were at the top of one of Chicago's skyscrapers, Travis couldn't remember the name. But all the walls were glass, and he could look out over the lights of the city.

It was a pretty view. Romantic. Except, there wasn't anything romantic about the evening. Not for him. He did see various men with their wives beside them. Women who were working the room by themselves, and other women who were obviously the power part of the power couple. Whose husbands stood quietly beside them, like scared mice.

He didn't want to be a husband like that, but he also wasn't entirely sure this was the place for him either.

And he longed to have Ellen beside him.

Of course he couldn't tell her that, couldn't even hint at it. But he'd already spilled a glass of something red and had accidentally stepped on someone's foot. Not because he was dancing, but just because he wasn't paying attention to what he was doing when he was backing up from the window view.

The woman whose foot he'd stepped on had been close to his age. She looked almost as uncomfortable as he did, which made him feel bad for her but not bad enough that he struck up a conversation.

He wasn't really interested in talking to people just for the sake of talking. He had some information Ford wanted him to find out, people Ford had suggested he casually acquaint himself with, and several other things that Ford had suggested he do.

So far, he'd checked three of the seven things off his list.

It was hard for him to feel inspired to do any more. He just... He couldn't find the inspiration. Hated the formality, hated the feeling of being trapped, both in his clothes and in the building. As pretty as the view was, it wasn't easy to get to the outside, and he had to swallow the panic that was probably instigated by a form of claustrophobia he didn't even realize he had.

He wasn't used to buildings where he couldn't get out within three to five seconds. How long did it take to run down the stairs and out the front door?

Here, one had to wait for an elevator, after one found the elevator, then one had to figure out how to maneuver out of the middle of the building to the outside, where one didn't run into grass but paved sidewalks and roads. An occasional tree was planted to give the illusion of... He wasn't even sure. Forest? Nature? There wasn't anything natural about a tree growing in cement.

Still, Ford was doing his best to try to teach him everything he needed to know in order to be successful for the rest of his life. He was taking a lot of time and a lot of energy and a lot of resources to make sure Travis didn't end up like the rest of his family, that he broke the cycle and was a good example to his brothers.

He couldn't let any of those people down, as much as he might hate it here.

Moving toward the bathroom, he found a quiet area and pulled the list he had made out of his pocket.

Too bad there wasn't a line for stepping on someone's toe or spilling a drink. He could check both of those two things off as well.

The lights weren't quite as bright and definitely not as fancy as he moved to the side while an older gentleman strode with purpose past him.

Shoving the list back in his pocket, he felt the letter from Ellen that he had just received on his way out the door brush his fingers.

He'd already read it three times and would have read it more, except he could hardly stand in a corner reading a letter when he was supposed to be mingling with the folks at the party.

It wouldn't hurt to take a couple of minutes break though, so he pulled it out, seeing the familiar handwriting on the outside of the envelope, running the tip of his finger over the letters, and thinking that Ellen had touched it, written those words, thought of him while she was writing his address.

So far away. A thousand miles? Something like that. In her home, with her uncle and his new wife, their baby, the animals around, cozy and snug and cool in the North Dakota summer.

Taking a breath, he pulled the letter out, opened it up, and cast a quick glance over his shoulder to make sure he was alone before he started to read.

Dear Travis,

I'm sorry that you're going to have to go to another black tie thing. I know you don't like them. But I'm glad that you're trusting Ford. I do know that he has your very best interest at heart. I heard Uncle Tadgh and him talking the other day, and I know they didn't think I could hear. I don't like to listen to people when they don't know I'm around, but I was working in Daisy's stall. She just had her fourth calf. You know we don't typically have our cows in, but Daisy is special. Usually she walks in the parade, and I wasn't sure Daisy was going to be able to, but she had her baby in time, and I figured that if I led Daisy, her little heifer, who I named Lily, would follow easily. So, I had Daisy in so I could clean her up when I had a few extra minutes.

Anyway, I was in her stall, teaching Lily to let me run my hands down her feet and under her belly, which seemed to tickle her because she kept moving away. That's when Uncle Tadgh and Ford walked in the barn.

Ford said that you are doing an ex-cellent job. He said he was impressed with how fast you're learning things and that he hadn't expected you to do so well. Uncle Tadgh told Ford that he hoped that you were a good influence on your brothers, because he was worried about Roger especially.

I don't think you need to worry about him, even though Uncle Tadgh said he was. It's mostly because he wants to sleep in on Sunday morning instead of go to church. Uncle Tadgh says that that's the first thing that happens when someone starts slipping away from the Lord. They fall out of church, they stop associating with other Christians, they quit reading the Bible, and then before they know it, they're just like the rest of the world, and there's no difference between them and someone who was raised on sitcoms and movies and Hollywood.

I know Uncle Tadgh knows what he's talking about, and I'm glad that he never let me sit around and stare at the TV set instead of going out and doing stuff. I wouldn't be here with three champion trophies on my windowsill from Chewy's herding competitions, and I wouldn't have trained her myself.

I'm sure you probably agree with that as well, because you can't let people who hate God fill your mind with junk if you want to point people to Jesus.

Also, as tempting as it is to just veg out, it's not good for your brain.

Uncle Tadgh says, and in my limited experience, I have to agree with him, that Hollywood doesn't love Jesus, and pretty much everything they make shows that in some way. Sometimes it's subtle, and we don't even realize we're being brainwashed. Like the frog that was put in the pot and the water just slowly gets warmer.

I suppose I'm not telling you anything you don't already know. You've been out and about in the world much more than I have. And I have to admit, I don't have any desire to leave Sweet Water. It's the best place in the world. I guess I understand how some people think that they want to make a big mark in the world so they need to go someplace big and do something big, but that's just not me. I... I don't have any desire to do anything like that. I just want to be here with my family, my dogs, my cows, and hang out with my sister, and just be a good example for her. I suppose people would say I have a lack of ambition, but my ambition is just to be someone who points other people to Jesus. Just where I am. You know that song "Brighten the Corner Where You Are"? That's me.

Anyway, this isn't a black tie affair, but Aunt Ashley wants me to go to prom. Three boys asked me, if you can imagine. I certainly was shocked when the first one asked, and then to have two more? It was pretty unbelievable. I said no to the first guy, but when I told Aunt Ashley about it, she said that I should go just as friends. She said I wouldn't regret the experience.

I know she knows what she's talking about, but it was hard to believe, and I still turned the second guy down. But when the third guy asked, I remembered what Aunt Ashley said, and I told him that I would go but I didn't want to hold his hand or kiss him or anything.

He laughed and said that maybe he could change my mind, which I didn't tell him, but I could assure him that my mind is not changing. Regardless, even though I have my driver's license and I told him I was quite capable of driving myself to the dance, he said he would come and pick me up. I guess I'll let him. Aunt Ashley said I probably should. Then she laughed, like the idea of me wanting to drive myself to the dance was funny.

I suppose it kind of is, but I'm not used to people doing things for me. I'm used to doing everything myself. Taking care of myself, figuring things out myself, you know, like you have to do whenever you're in a competition with your dog and something goes wrong. There isn't anybody to tell you what to do, you have to figure it out on your own.

Anyway, I guess I have to let this guy come pick me up and spend the evening with him thinking that he's going to somehow magically convince me that I should let him kiss me. Fat chance.

Anyway, that's all that's happening here, and by the time you get this letter, I'll probably already have been at the dance. It's this Friday night.

I hope you have a good week, and I hope you don't suffocate in your tux. I know you hate them.

Take care, my friend.

Ellen

Travis shoved the letter back in his pocket, pressing his lips together.

It had been his idea to be just friends. He'd said it with the idea that Ellen would probably date other boys, and that if he waited, he might lose her.

He hadn't realized how hard it was going to be. He didn't want to lose her. Didn't want to have to wait. Couldn't stand the idea of her going to prom with someone else.

But she was still only sixteen, and he still was too old for her. Plus, he was in Chicago and would be stuck there for another few years.

The rest of the night dragged by, although he did manage to check off everything on the list that Ford had given him.

He made it back to his apartment, exhausted in body but with his mind churning.

He didn't even try to go to bed, but pulled his notebook out, and started to write.

> Dear Ellen,
>
> I want to quit.
>
> Feels like I'm not learning anything, not doing anything, not going any-where, while I'm missing all the things that I want to do and learn and be. I miss Sweet Water, I long for it with a physical feeling I can't even describe. That makes me want to walk out the door right now and just start walking home, if that's what it'll take to get me there.

I hate it here. I've tried to look on the bright side, tried to think about all the positives, but that's the bottom line. I wouldn't admit that to just anyone, and I shouldn't be admitting it to you now.

I'm not cut out to be a businessman. I don't enjoy any of the things that have anything to do with it, and I wish I wouldn't have come. I don't want to let Ford down, but that's probably the only thing keeping me here. I want to go home.

Sorry, I know you don't really need me dumping on you, but I just had a miserable night, and I knew you'd understand.

Your friend,

Travis

Chapter 20

Ellen stared at the letter she just opened. She hadn't even waited to get to the house, but grabbed it at the mailbox, ran to the barn, and sat in Daisy's stall while she read it.

She couldn't let Travis quit. He needed to do this. He needed to stick it out. If he came home, he would always regret quitting, would feel like a failure, would think he was a quitter.

Jumping up and grabbing the notebook that she kept to write down the information she needed to keep track of with her animals, she flipped to the first blank page, grabbed the pencil that sat beside it, and hurried back to Daisy's stall to write back. If she was quick, she might be able to get the letter into the post office in Sweet Water so it would go out that very day.

Dear Travis,

I know you're discouraged, and I know it seems like nothing is happening, but I wanted to encourage you not to quit. I know you probably figured it out by now, and I know you know this anyway, but God has you there for a reason. And you committed to it. You don't want to go back on your commitment. Not unless there's no other way. After all, when you can't go forward, sometimes you have to go sideways, or over or under, and sometimes backward. And that's understandable. But you can't allow yourself to get discouraged and give up. You know you won't be able to live with yourself if you do that.

You know you will regret it.

Of course, I'll still be your friend whatever you decide, no matter what, but just remember, if you quit and then change your mind, it's always harder to go back. People don't trust you anymore.

Sometimes when I think that something is too hard, I stop looking at the big picture and just focus on the one thing I can do. I wanted to win a championship with Chewy, but training her was hard and it seemed like it was too much for me. So, I just did something little every day. Ten minutes of training. And I made it fun. I have to make things fun, or I have trouble getting myself to do them.

I don't always like mucking out stalls or getting up before daylight when it's below zero and I have to go outside, but I just tell myself stories in my head, or I remind myself how this is making me a stronger, better person. I don't see myself getting stronger and better, but I can sometimes stop and look back and see how far I've come. Maybe you need to do this? Think about your mom and your homelife here and how what you're doing now is going to help you and change the lives of your brothers and your whole family.

I wish there was something I could do, some way I could come out and encourage you. But you know I'm behind you, you know I pray for you every day, and you know that if there's anything that you need, anything that I can do, I'll do it.

This morning when I got up, I made chocolate chip cookies, just because my little sister loves them. And I wanted to do it before it got too hot out. I am going to pack some up and send them to you. They'll hopefully be a little taste of home in a place that doesn't feel that way. Maybe the smell will make it more cozy for you. I know the smell of chocolate chip cookies always makes me smile.

Anyway, everyone says you're doing a great job. It might not feel like you are, and you might not see results right away, but let me encourage you to just stick with it. I know that eventually your time is going to come.

All right, I'm gonna run in and start packing up my cookies. Take care, and you know I'm here anytime you need me.

Ellen

Chapter 21

"**A**re you sure that your parents are going to be okay with this?" Toni whispered as a knock sounded on the diner door.

"They're fine with it. We talked to them, and they laughed a little, shook their heads, then said that people had done similar things to them, and everything worked out."

"All right. If you're sure." Toni bit her lip uncertainly.

They had announced in church this morning that they were going to have a cooking class. Mr. Blaze and Mr. Junior had been growing more and more mo-rose since Mr. Marshall had gotten mar-ried and moved to Good Grief, Idaho.

But Toni and her friends had figured out that it wasn't just because Mr. Mar-shall had moved away. It was because they were lonely.

Their mom was too busy to offer cook-ing classes at the diner anymore. Her Marry Me Chicken had gotten so popu-lar that she had to hire a whole crew of workers and expand the kitchen in the back. Now, people worked just to put the Marry Me Chicken together and ship it out.

She and their dad had been talking about setting up business in an actual factory, but they were afraid they would lose quality.

So for now, the prices were a little higher, but the quality was as high as they could make it as well.

Regardless, with all that going on, their mom hadn't offered cooking classes for the residents of Sweet Water for years, but Sorrell and Merritt and herself had never forgotten that the three old coots had done their very best to get their moms matched up and to give them dads.

They had been a little discouraged that Mr. Marshall was the only one that they had been able to match of the three old coots.

So, when they invited them to attend a cooking class, they didn't tell them that they had already issued specific invitations to the Benson twins who lived just outside of town.

Both of them had become widows in the last five years, and they'd moved in together.

At seventy-eight, they felt like they were too young for a nursing home or even assisted living center, but they were also too old to live by themselves.

Regardless, Sorrell and Toni had talked about it and decided that the Benson twins were perfect for Mr. Blaze and Mr. Junior.

Still, just because they were perfect for them didn't make it easy to try to figure out how to get them together.

The cooking lessons were the only thing they could think of.

"I think I hear someone knocking on the door. Should I get it?" Sally said, coming around the corner from the kitchen. Sally was easy to tell from her sister Sadie, since she was the one who had her nose pierced.

Sadie's hair was pink on one side and blue on the other, soft colors that went well with the white roots and made her head look similar to cotton candy.

The girls were talking beside the bar and hadn't made a move to walk to the front door. The blinds were drawn, so whoever was knocking couldn't see inside, and Toni took the last second to check and make sure it was what they really wanted to do.

So many times, the thing she tried to do had gone horribly wrong, and she didn't want her mom to be disappointed in her.

Not that her mom ever was, it was just something she worked hard to avoid.

"No, it's okay, you can go back to the kitchen and make sure you and Sadie have your hairnets on. I'll get the door," Merritt said, confident as she stepped out and walked to the door.

With her hand on the knob, she looked back over her shoulder and said in a stage whisper to Toni, "Everything is going to be okay. Trust me."

"You know, the Marry Me Chicken actually worked out pretty well for us," Sorrell said, still standing beside Toni. But she spoke low, just in case Merritt opened the door.

"I know. You're right. And things worked out really well for me. I have the best dad in the world, and I even have siblings now. It's been really great."

"And we want Mr. Blaze and Mr. Junior to be matched up. This is the best way to do it. And if it doesn't work, we'll figure something else out!" Sorrell held her hands out like they could have come up with a million ideas and could try them all.

She was probably mostly right, except Toni didn't want to hurt anyone. She couldn't think of how this would be painful to anyone, so she decided that she just needed to stop worrying and trust her friends.

"Mr. Blaze! Mr. Junior! Come on in. I'm sorry that it's been so long since we've had cooking lessons. I'm so glad you guys are still interested."

"Not interested so much, we're just tired of the same old same old. We need to learn something new. Kinda given up on TikTok, but I suppose we could revive the old channel. Except, things just aren't the same without Mr. Marshall around." Mr. Blaze sounded a little depressed, and Toni was glad that they decided to do this. If anything, he needed a little pick-me-up, and this should do it for them. Even if nothing ever came out of it.

"We're fine without him. Better off even," Mr. Junior said, although his voice lacked any kind of conviction. "I'm tired of eating my own cooking too. But no more TikTok for me. All that did was bring orange-haired women into our lives and stole our friend away."

He didn't seem to notice that the end of his sentence contradicted the begin-ning. Maybe that was how she would be when she was eighty, Toni wasn't sure.

At any rate, Merritt waited until they walked through the door and then closed it. Although before it clicked entirely shut, she paused and looked back over her shoulder. "Is that Billy? What's he doing here?"

"He followed us down the street. Got a little annoyed when he thought we were going to walk by the diner. It's like he thought you guys were open or something, and he's herding people in. Are you paying him to do that?" Mr. Blaze said, seeming to realize how ridiculous he sounded when he said that the steer was herding them into the diner. Like Billy might know whether or not it was open.

Toni's eyes got big, and she gave Sorrell a look.

Sorrell didn't really return it though. She acted like she believed the steer might actually be doing some match-making. It was a rumor that had been going around town for years, but no one ever put any stock in the idea that it could actually be true. Steers were just dumb animals that had no actual brain. They didn't match people up. They couldn't even tell whether a person was a man or a woman or married or unmarried.

The idea didn't make any sense at all, but Toni supposed people believed what they wanted to believe, whether or not it had any resemblance to actual truth.

She had to keep that in mind, because it could just as easily be her who was fooled as someone else.

She didn't want to believe things that weren't true. That was why her mom was always trying to get her to match things up with the Bible. If someone said something, no matter how reasonable it sounded, it didn't matter, not if it didn't line up with what Scripture said. After all, God didn't have to make sense, since He was God.

So many times, it seemed like people wanted to explain things away, just so they could have whatever it was they wanted.

This whole matchmaking thing seemed like one of those things to Toni, but she didn't really think the Bible had too much to say about steers and their ability to play Cupid. So, it was something that didn't matter in the long run.

Otherwise, God would have made a law about it or given them a command in the Bible.

He also didn't say anything about locking people in a diner for an afternoon, just to see if they couldn't get them to get married.

While it didn't seem like it was totally on the up-and-up, there was still no biblical law against it, and that was the only thing she was going to be able to say to her mom if she got in trouble for it. God didn't say no, so I figured it was okay.

She wasn't sure that argument was going to hold any water, but as much as her mom quoted Scripture and told her about God's laws and not disobeying them, she figured it was as good a shot as any.

"All right, all the ingredients that you need and the recipe itself for the meal are on the counter in the kitchen. My friends and I are going to go." Merritt said this cheerfully, like this was what happened every time they went to cooking class.

"Oh." She stopped in the process of linking her arms with Sorrell and Toni to turn and look back at Mr. Blaze and Mr. Junior who had shocked looks on their faces. "In case you didn't notice when you walked in, we switched the doorknobs, so the locks are on the inside. If you have an extreme emergency, you can call us, but otherwise, we expect you to be here at nine o'clock this evening when we'll come in to let you out."

That was all she said before she finished grabbing Toni's arm and led her sister and Toni out the door, closing it behind them. The old men found their voices just before the door closed, and they could hear both of them in the background telling them to wait and asking them what in the world they were talking about.

They would find the Benson twins in the kitchen soon enough, and whatever the four of them decided to do from then on was totally up to them.

Sure enough, Billy stood on the sidewalk as Toni and her friends paused on the other side of the door.

They'd drawn the blinds on purpose so people couldn't see what havoc they created.

"I think Billy approves," Sorrell said with a smile in her voice.

"I'm sure my mother doesn't," Toni muttered.

"You told me yourself that the Bible did not forbid this, but come on, we don't want to be standing in front of the door in case they come over and pull the blinds. Let's go!" Merritt said, pulling on their arms, and soon they were racing down the sidewalk, turning the corner, and heading toward the new park.

Toni had certainly never pictured herself as a kidnapper, but that's kind of how she felt.

Chapter 22

Blaze stared at the door. They locked it? He could see that they indeed had turned the knob around, and the keycode was on this side of the door.

Still, he couldn't stop himself from going over to try the door.

"They didn't lie. It's locked." He turned to Junior, confusion on his face. "I can't believe they did that. I... I didn't think those girls were the kind of people to play pranks like that."

"Well, at least they didn't leave us without food. They said all the ingredients are in the kitchen. And maybe they forgot to lock the other door."

Blaze figured they probably didn't forget. If they took the time to switch the knob on the front door completely around so that the outside was inside, they probably didn't forget to lock the back door. But he supposed it was possible.

He shrugged his shoulders. "I guess we can check."

He wasn't totally upset. After all, he didn't have any other plans for today, it was just... He felt a little betrayed by the girls. He thought they were...friends, if it was possible for teenagers to be friends with men who were pushing eighty years old.

But as they opened the door to the kitchen and saw the Benson twins, of all people, standing in the kitchen, Blaze began to think that maybe the girls weren't doing it to be unkind.

"What are you two doing here?" Junior said, as soon as he saw the ladies in the kitchen.

Blaze shook his head. Junior had no idea how to be subtle. "Good afternoon, ladies. What a lovely day for a cooking class. It's unfortunate that our hosts seem to have disappeared."

The ladies looked up, and Sally, her nose ring glinting in the sun and the overhead florescent light, like it was w inking directly at Blaze, kind of flirting, sa id, "What are you doing here?" emphasizing the "you."

Sadie, her cotton candy hair looking slightly more garish under the harsh lights, glanced at Blaze. "Our hosts? You mean the girls? Where are they? What did you do with them?" she finally asked in a strident voice, her hands on her hips. "If you hurt them, so help me, I've got a cane and I'm not afraid to use it."

"I have a cane of my own. If I'd have known we were going to have sword fights, I would have brought it," Blaze said, irritated that she would assume that he would actually do something to harm those sweet girls. Of course, he wasn't thinking they were so sweet just a couple of minutes ago, but still, it was the idea.

Junior had already gone through and checked the back door. "It's locked, the locks are backward, just like the front door. We're stuck here." He came back to the kitchen and slapped the counter. "I would never have thought the girls would do this to us."

Blaze, realizing Junior still hadn't figured things out, tried to say in an aside, which was hard to do since Junior was further away from him than either of the Benson twins. He could only hope they forgot to put their hearing aids in this morning before they showed up to the diner.

"Junior. We might be stuck here, but we have…good…company." He tried to put a little spin on the word "good" and make it say something along the lines of, "we're here with two ladies our age, they are unmarried, we're unmarried, and this is the opportunity of a lifetime. The girls have done us a favor, they haven't done anything unkind, actually given us the opportunity that we've been looking for. Don't screw this up, buddy."

He wasn't quite sure whether he was successful in getting all that in his tone or not, but he tried.

Junior didn't seem like he understood anything, just stood across the kitchen, his brows bent down, his face showing

that he had no clue what Blaze was saying.

"We're stuck with these ladies. They are
single, we are single. Let's make the best
of it." Blaze finally decided he might
as well just spit it out. He didn't have
anything to lose, and it wasn't like he
didn't have the rest of the afternoon to
try to figure out how to take his foot
out of his mouth. That was one of the
benefits of being stuck with a woman
who couldn't get away from a person.
He had a chance to correct his mistakes.
And the competition wasn't super fierce.
After all, he was just in here with Junior,
and Junior had already shown that he
wasn't exactly the brightest bulb in the
pack.

"Now, ladies, looks like we're stuck here together for a while, how about we talk about getting married."

That was a pretty good opening line, if Blaze did say so himself.

The ladies looked less than impressed though, since they seemed to be just figuring out what he had known now for at least three minutes, and that was that they were stuck in here together.

"What do you mean stuck?" Sally said, her face pinching, like she didn't like the idea.

"I mean the doors are locked, and unless we're going to break a window, we can't get out. The girls did say they would unlock the door tonight by nine o'clock. I think they're expecting us to be engaged by then, and we can probably go see the preacher if we managed to get there by midnight. What do you say?" He directed that last question to Junior, who finally seemed to be getting with the program.

"Hold on here a second. You're saying the girls did this on purpose?"

"Yep."

"To get us married?"

"Yup."

"To the Benson twins?"

"Yep."

"I see." Junior's eyes slid across the room and landed on the two ladies who stood shoulder to shoulder.

Blaze wasn't entirely sure, but he thought they were warming up to the idea.

Once a person hit seventy, a lifetime vow wasn't quite as big of a deal as it was when a person was twenty. At least in his eyes. After all, after seventy, he was only looking at a couple decades tops, maybe three, where at twenty, a lifetime vow would be more than twice that long.

"All right, folks. It's like this. We're not getting any younger here. The girls did us a favor, and we need to step up to the plate."

"What in the world are you talking about?" Sally said, glaring at him. Her hands on her hips, her head tilted toward her sister, like she was going to protect her at all costs.

"I know it's not the most romantic thing in the world, but time is short. Do you want to take a chance, or don't you?" Blaze said.

Junior held up his hand. "He gets ahead of himself sometimes, ladies. But what he's saying is he'd like to cook with you. He'd enjoy your company, and he thinks spending the afternoon locked in the diner with two lovely ladies such as yourselves is about the best thing that has happened to him in the last ten years."

Junior lifted his brows at Blaze. "Right?" He said that with a special emphasis in his voice that Blaze couldn't quite figure out.

But it wasn't hard to see what Junior was doing. Instead of reminding the women how old they were and how little time they had, he was remembering what they learned all of their lives. Women didn't like to be grabbed like a flapjack, they wanted to be treated like they were special, valuable, and important.

Blaze hadn't forgotten that; he just got caught up in the idea that he didn't have much time left, so he was always pushing things, too much probably.

Now that he was older, he should have more patience, not less.

Taking a breath and lifting his chin, he looked at the ladies. "I do believe my dear friend is correct. We have lovely company, delicious food, and a wonderful recipe. Would you be interested in spending the afternoon with us, figuring this out, and making ourselves a delectable meal that we can share in a leisurely manner together?"

Even if it took a little longer, this was probably the better way. He definitely liked the expression on the ladies' faces much better as they nodded their heads and smiled with anticipation.

Chapter 23

Miller walked out into the yard, holding his coffee cup. The rain from the evening before had washed everything clean, the grass seemed to sparkle, the buildings even glittered, and the smell of fresh, clean earth was heavy in the air.

He loved mornings after it rained, where everything seemed fresh and new and the thirsty grasses were still heavy with moisture and the colors sparkled in the early rays of sun.

Of course, the sun coming over the horizon had a tendency to touch everything with its glow. Still, there was just something beautiful about the morning.

He laughed at himself. He almost seemed like a romantic fool. It might not be the sun or the morning or the rain at all, and just the fact that he'd stood in the shed with Carna, talking to her and having a great time. Such a nice time that he'd...asked her out on a date?

He hoped that wasn't what it was, since they'd just ridden in his truck to the diner and grabbed supper. The diner had been busy, but they'd scored the back table, and they'd not been bothered at all, even when the ladies they'd led on a trail ride had come in after them. They'd waved, but that was it. Danielle looked annoyed the one time he glanced at her, but he didn't look at her again because he'd been too busy talking and laughing with Carna.

It had been a fun supper, and he'd enjoyed it.

Maybe he enjoyed it a little too much, since he fell asleep thinking about her and woke up doing the same.

"Good morning," Smith said as he walked toward him, carrying his own coffee cup and strolling, as Smith often did in the morning. Miller kinda figured it was his prayer time, but Smith never seemed like it was a bother to be interrupted on the mornings that Miller met him on his stroll.

"Beautiful morning," Miller commented in what he figured was a casual tone as he took a sip of his coffee.

"Same as yesterday," Smith said, tilting his head and looking at Miller as though he'd caught something in his tone that was a little bit unusual.

"It's always pretty after rain," Miller said, hoping he wasn't digging the hole deeper, instead of getting himself out.

"It is?" Smith asked, looking around as though he'd never noticed that the world shimmered more when it had been washed by rain. His eyes narrowed as he looked back at Miller. "Is it the rain? Or is it something else?"

"The rain," Miller said, choking a bit on his coffee and taking another gulp to wash it down.

That backfired, and he ended up getting more in his lungs, coughing, and spending the next thirty seconds in a coughing fit.

"I learned the Heimlich years ago in a class they gave us in the Air Force. I never thought I would have to use it on someone choking on their morning coffee," Smith murmured with a hand on Miller's back, looking with concern, as Miller finally stopped coughing.

"I don't think I need the Heimlich," Miller murmured, clearing his throat once more and still feeling like he didn't quite get all the coffee out of his lungs.

Hopefully, he struggled enough that Smith had totally forgotten what they were talking about.

"It's Carna, isn't it?"

Well, so much for thinking positively.

"What is?" Miller asked, clearing his throat a little harder than necessary and throwing in another cough, just for good measure.

"When you meet someone, sometimes it makes the world seem like a better place. I think that's what's happened to you. At least, that's what my wife said."

"You need to stop talking to your wife so much," Miller muttered.

"I'll tell her you said that." Smith laughed.

"No. Don't. She cooks my lunch most of the time. I would hate to get shut off from the table. After all, I kinda depend on that for supper too."

"If you get married... Well, with Carna, things might not change in that area if you get married." Smith laughed like that was hilarious.

"Carna... She's your sister, for one."

"So?"

"Well, that's just, she's your sister. And, I mean, I guess she's grown up a little since I knew her last—"

"I knew you noticed. Okay, you're kinda confirming everything I just said."

"Would you stop twisting what I'm telling you?"

"I mention Carna, and you come out fighting. Just stop it. There's no point."

"No point in fighting? Wait. I'm not fighting. I'm just telling you why you're wrong."

"You're wasting your breath. I'm not wrong, we both know it, so stop."

"Since when did you become such an expert on relationships?" Miller finally said in frustration. Smith wasn't listening, wouldn't accept his disagreement, and was being frustrating.

"I'm just telling you what my wife said. And she's never wrong. So, just accept the inevitable."

"It is not inevitable. I'm not accepting anything. Carna is a nice girl, but that's it. She isn't making the sun shine bright or the roses bloom or whatever it was that you were saying."

"You were the one saying it, and it was how she was making the morning beautiful."

"Fine. It's a nasty morning, and I hate my life. Is that better?" He shook his head, started stalking away, then stopped. "You have work for me to do today? Or should I just go stew in my misery? Since you can't seem to stand anyone who is happy."

"Well, as much as it pains me to do it, I'm going to have to send you on the crop-dusting crew. You'll be out for three days. I know, it's terrible, you're going to miss Carna considerably, but you're just going to have to suck it up. Then, once you come back, it will be time for you guys to go to the competition."

Miller decided to just ignore everything he was saying about Carna. Smith wasn't accepting Miller's protestations of innocence, and there was no point fighting about it.

"What exactly are we supposed to be doing for the competition? You do know your sister had never ridden a horse?" He hated for Carna to get hurt doing something she didn't have any experience in.

"Oh. That's too bad. I suppose if you had been able to stick around for the next three days, you could have given her some riding lessons yourself."

"You're hilarious. No. In fact, never mind. I don't really care whether she can ride a horse or not."

There he was, getting all upset again, just because Smith was needling him. It was annoying. Why couldn't he just stay cool like he always did?

"Anyway. You're the one who wants to win the competition to bring attention to the ranch because we need the money. If you don't care whether she can ride or rope or do anything that she'll probably be asked to do in the competition, that's up to you. I'm just letting you know."

"Actually, I don't know what's going to happen in the competition. It's a sur-prise to everyone. That way, people can't send folks who are good at whatever they're going to have you do. So, it says in the instructions that they could have you cooking or chopping firewood or plowing a field. It just depends."

"Depends on what?"

"I guess what they decide. It says that they're not letting anyone know; you'll find out when you get there. It's making for a more intriguing contest. From what I understand, they haven't had any trouble selling tickets."

"Probably what they're having trouble with is getting contestants. Who wants to go somewhere where you don't know what you're doing? I could end up having to sew a dress or something. That would be a little awkward."

"Especially if Carna had to wear it. She might not be very appreciative of me by the time she gets back here." Smith laughed again, then he walked over and slapped Miller on the shoulder. "My wife assures me that both of you are going to be very appreciative that we sent you away together by the time you return."

Miller opened his mouth to protest, but Smith continued, "My wife is never wrong."

That was just great.

"I think I'll leave right now for that three-day trip. It's looking really good to me."

He stomped off as Smith called after him, "You can leave just as soon as the tanks are filled so you can gas up. Truck's coming at nine."

That was not soon enough. Hopefully he could manage to avoid Carna for that long. Although, that thought was shattered when Smith called, "Carna is taking care of the horses for you while you're gone. Make sure she knows how."

That was just great.

Chapter 24

arna set the cooler on the ground beside the stable door.

She had the ice packs in the freezer and would add the last of them when Miller got home.

He'd been gone for three days on some kind of crop-dusting run. She wasn't even sure where he went, other than he was going to be flying an airplane. Which w as dangerous, and for some odd reason, s he was a little bit afraid. Worried maybe.

She did more praying than she normally did, and she wasn't even sure why.

After all, Miller's safety had never bothered her overly much before.

Maybe it was the time in the shed with the rain coming down and feeling like they were cocooned in their own little world. Maybe it was realizing that he wasn't the self-centered teenager he used to be.

She had been self-centered as well, and it hadn't been a shock to realize she'd grown up. But... She just expected him to stay the same.

But he hadn't. And she found herself thinking about him more and more to her consternation, since she didn't want to.

Lord, keep Miller safe.

The prayer came unbidden to her heart again, and she whispered it, thinking about his whispered name, her heartfelt plea, going up before the throne of the Father, and of God watching Miller and keeping His hand of protection on him.

Maybe that wasn't how it worked, but it was what was in her mind. And in her heart.

She'd taken care of the horses exactly as he had said, even though he'd been in a rush the morning he'd told her how. He said he'd just found out he was leaving, so it made sense that he couldn't take much time, and if he'd been a little brusque, it was probably because he didn't want to go on such short notice.

She hadn't allowed it to bother her, since they'd agreed to call a truce.

Trying to think if there was anything else she might need to take to the competition, she straightened and looked around the stable.

"You all packed?"

She jumped, Abrielle's voice startling her.

"Yeah. I think so. I was just trying to decide if there was anything else we needed."

Abrielle had a hand on her back and one on her stomach. Her baby wasn't due for a while yet, but it seemed like a lot of work to carry a little one around all the time.

Abrielle often looked tired, but she usually looked happy with a happy kind of tired that made Carna think that maybe the work wasn't as odious as it could have been.

"I just talked to Smith, and he said that Miller would be here within the next thirty minutes. I wanted to make sure you were good."

They had just seen each other at lunch, so it was a little bit odd that Abrielle had sought her out, although maybe she wanted to talk privately.

"I think I am. I wish that we knew what we were doing, but I understand the draw of making it all a surprise. That's actually a pretty good idea."

She was a lot more nervous than what she wanted to admit. She hadn't told anyone else at the ranch that she wasn't able to ride, or rope, or pretty much do anything that a cowboy was expected to do.

Smith already knew, and if he put her down for the competition knowing that, then she supposed he was more interested in something besides her skills on a horse and ranch.

She could milk a cow with the best of them, and while she didn't particularly care for driving tractors, she was skilled at it.

She'd even fixed things, although electricity made her nervous. Still, being nervous didn't get a person out of a job that needed to be done, especially one that needed to be done in order for eighty cows to get milked, so she learned to suck it up and do it anyway.

Maybe that was the quality he was looking for. Someone who would suck it up and do it anyway.

That was her.

She almost laughed, because that was probably her top skill. Not roping or riding or anything that most people thought of when they thought of ranch work. Her ability was just digging in and doing it, sticking with it until it was finished, no matter how long it took or how hard it was or how successful she was. She didn't quit.

She sighed. Why couldn't she possess talent for something helpful?

"I guess I was talking more about being with Miller. Smith said you two didn't get along very well when you were younger, and I wanted to make sure you were okay with being at the competition for three days with him. Not that I can really change it now, but... I just thought I'd ask," Abrielle finished lamely, almost as though she wasn't quite sure what she was trying to say.

"I don't know. We seemed like we were getting along okay, but just before he left, he was giving me instructions about the horses and he was...rather distant." That was putting it mildly. She thought that their relationship, such as it was, took a giant step forward when they spent the hour or so in the shed with the rain. It had been one of the best hours of her life, which was sad but totally true.

They'd had a great time at the diner afterward, laughing like they were old friends rather than old enemies.

Still, the next day, Miller had acted like it had never happened. Or like he wanted it to have never happened. She wasn't sure which, he'd just been very brief when he gave her instructions about the horses, and it was like he couldn't get away from her fast enough.

He hadn't taken his dog, and Pepper had taken to following her around. Or maybe he was following Posey. She wasn't sure, but both of them were lying in a corner just five yards away from where she was.

If she were to walk across the yard to the house, they would follow and both of them would lie on the porch waiting for her to come out.

Hopefully when Miller got back, his dog would go back to following him. She didn't want him to be mad at her because she somehow stole his dog away.

That wasn't what she was trying to do.

A horse neighed, and Abrielle looked over. "Is that Fancy?" she asked, going over and looking over the top of the half door.

"No. I have Fancy and her filly out in the field. That's Monday. She's due anytime, according to Miller. He gave me a bunch of things to watch for, and I feel like she's not going to have it today."

"That's good to know. It would be nice if it came when Miller is here. He spent so much time with the horses, and he loves them."

Abrielle ran her hand down Monday's neck, whispering to the horse and adjusting her mane.

Carna figured that Abrielle had an affinity with the pregnant mare.

"So what do you think of Miller?" Abrielle asked, and it seemed like an innocent question, except it came out of the blue and kind of surprised Carna, and she figured it probably wasn't that innocent.

"When we were younger, we hated each other, but now we're kinda getting along. Like I just said."

"I know. You'd said that you guys were getting along okay, but I'm asking… What do you think of him?"

"I think he used to be a spoiled, self-centered jerk, but… I don't think he's that anymore."

"What is he now?"

"He seems to have character. Integrity. He… When we went on the trail ride, one of the girls was flirting with him. He wasn't unkind to her, but he didn't flirt back. It was like… Like he knew he needed to be nice for the sake of the ranch, but he had enough self-control to not… I don't know how to say it, but I was impressed."

"I see. Well, he is a very, very eligible cowboy and a big draw for any of the Eastern girls that we get."

"Western girls too, I'm sure."

"Yeah. I'm sure there's been some local girls who are interested as well. Are you?"

That last question took Carna by surprise.

"No!" she said immediately, but she wasn't entirely sure that was true. She tried to temper her response with things she was absolutely certain of. "I'm not interested in getting married. Obviously. I... I'm looking pretty hard at thirty, and yet... I don't have a house, I don't even own a bed. All I have is my car. I feel like I've worked for the last decade or so and don't have anything to show for it. I'm...definitely not ready to get married."

"Does everything have to be perfect before you can get married?"

"I wouldn't want to marry someone like me. Someone who is almost thirty and doesn't even have a home. I live in a stable, for goodness' sake."

"Would it make you feel better if you had a room in the house?"

"First of all, I couldn't do that. And secondly, no. It's not that it makes me feel bad, it's just... I don't know. It feels like I'm not a responsible adult to have not done more with my life so far."

"Did you help your grandparents?"

"Yes."

"They needed someone on the farm, and you stepped up. It wasn't your fault the farm was in financial trouble. You stuck with your grandparents, even though you knew you weren't gaining anything. Probably most of the time, you didn't get paid."

"That's true."

"And yet you stayed. You did...what some people might call your duty by your family, but I don't really think you saw it as a duty. You lived your love. It sounds a little corny, but isn't that what happened? You love your family, you say you'll do anything for them, but some people say that, and then when push comes to shove, they don't actually do anything at all. You on the other hand didn't just say you love them, you showed that love. Maybe you don't have any material things to show for your life, but you have a legacy of showing your love. Of living what you believe. Of sacrificing and working and giving, even when there's no benefit to yourself."

Carna stood speechless. She hadn't considered it like that at all. She wasn't really disappointed with the way her life turned out, she just knew she wasn't considered a catch by any stretch of the imagination. She wasn't beautiful, she didn't dress in anything but boots, jeans, and T-shirts, and she didn't have social graces or anything else, add that to the fact that all she owned was her car and a dog she inherited, and that was pretty much it.

She hadn't thought of her life in the terms that Abrielle had just laid out.

"Thanks for saying that. I guess you made me think of things in a slightly different way. I still don't know if I'm ready to get married," she laughed a little, "but I guess you maybe see that the things that I've done with my life are things that are eternal, not things that are temporal, like a house or possessions."

"Exactly. And there's plenty of room here. So you have a place on the ranch as long as you want, because Smith is your brother, and that's just the way we roll."

"I never doubted it. And I'm happy here. I'm happy living above the stables. I didn't mean to imply that I wasn't." And that was true. Her room was cozy and just what she needed, and even if she had to share the kitchen with Miller... She hadn't really thought about that. She didn't mind sharing a kitchen or the bathroom, since she actually kind of liked Miller. Except, he acted like he didn't want to like her half the time.

"Miller seemed a little bit confused before he left. Smith had talked to him, and I think he likes you. But I think maybe he doesn't want to. I'm not sure why."

"We have history." She shrugged her shoulder, although she didn't really believe that Miller liked her, like a romantic like. He was probably just struggling with the idea that he didn't even want to be friends with her.

"I don't think that's it. I think Miller was like you. He wasn't planning on getting married, and he thought he was safe out here. Safe from women, I guess. But you're just the kind of woman he needs. I... I have a feeling that this trip could be life-changing for both of you. But I don't think that Miller realizes it. I just... Women seem to be a little bit more astute, and I wanted you to know that Smith and I are rooting for you."

Carna froze, her eyes wide, then she slowly drew back, and took a step back.

"Rooting for me?" She narrowed her eyes. "You mean like you're rooting for us to win the competition?"

"Well yeah, of course. But I meant rooting for you and Miller. The two of you belong together."

"We do?" she asked, unable to keep the disbelief out of her voice.

A noise drew her attention to the opening at the end of the stables.

There was an outline of a figure, black against the daylight. His face in shadow, his stance wide, a bag in his hand.

He just stood there, like maybe he'd heard the last part of the conversation and was as flabbergasted as Carna was.

They weren't exactly enemies, but they definitely weren't a couple. And they wouldn't be.

It felt like a year but was probably only a matter of seconds before the figure moved, and Miller stepped into the stables, walking with purpose toward the stairs.

"I need a shower, then I'm going to check the horses, then I'm ready to go. You packed?" His words were clipped, his sentences short, and he didn't do more than glance in her direction.

"I'm ready when you are."

She lifted her brows at Abrielle, almost as though to say that whatever Abrielle was trying to say that there could be between Miller and her was a figment of someone's imagination, since Miller was obviously not the slightest bit interested and actually seemed to be a little bit annoyed that he was going to have to go anywhere with her.

Abrielle patted Monday's neck, then she smiled at Carna. The door slammed closed above them.

"I don't think I'm wrong." Abrielle lifted her brows, as though giving Carna a little bit of encouragement, then she said, "I hope you have a safe trip. Don't put too much pressure on yourself to win. I think the idea is more to charm the crowd."

As she walked away, Carna realized maybe that was her intention after all. Maybe she was not exactly trying to get Miller and Carna together as much as she was trying to endear them to each other somehow so that they would play for the crowd better.

It was an interesting strategy but one that Carna had trouble wrapping her mind around.

Abrielle wanted the best for her, she was sure. And Smith was her brother. They both wanted the best for Miller as well, since he was a very good friend of theirs. There was no way that they were going to manipulate their personal lives just to win a contest.

Except the ranch was riding on it.

Surely his friend and his sister were more important to Smith than the ranch.

If that was the case, then Smith and Abrielle must really think that the best thing that could happen to Miller and Carna would be for them to get together.

That thought alone was enough for her to give credence to what Abrielle had been saying.

Was there attraction on Miller's part? Was he interested?

And for the last few years, when she had known with certainty that it was only a matter of time before she had to sell her grandparents' farm and lose everything that she had been working toward, she had questioned God. Why? Why had He allowed that to happen? Why had He taken the farm away from her? Wasn't hard work supposed to pay off? Wasn't a person supposed to reap what they sowed? Wasn't she supposed to work hard and see the results from that? She put in so much time and effort and sacrificed years of her life, and yet they'd lost the farm anyway.

Was it all part of God's plan? His plan to move her out West, to live with her brother, to meet Miller, to...fall in love?

Except, she wasn't even close to falling in love. She wasn't even sure whether she was in like with him.

Except, that little bit of time in the shed had been really nice.

Okay, she wasn't sure exactly what Abrielle's intention had been, but she had succeeded in making Carna think that maybe there could be more to Miller and her than grudging friendship.

Maybe this trip would show them exactly what that could be.

Chapter 25

Miller stood watching the horses for a lot longer time than what he needed to. Fancy and her foal were doing just fine, and although watching the antics of the foal galloping around the pasture, zipping and zagging, with her mom as her fulcrum was adorable, and he could stand and watch for hours, it wasn't getting him to where he needed to go.

It was helping him calm down a little.

He'd missed Carna.

Funny how someone who hadn't even been back in his life for long at all had somehow wormed her way into having him care about her.

In the three days he'd spent working, he convinced himself that she cared about him. After all, she hadn't been in a big rush to leave the shed. She'd been content to stand beside him. To talk to him. She had acted like she hated him, but when they were in the shed and at the diner, he'd thought...maybe she liked him a little.

Maybe she was even a little jealous. She claimed she wasn't, and he believed her, but maybe it just bothered her some that there was someone else who was interested in him.

Not that he was under any illusions about that woman's interest. He couldn't even remember her name. She just wanted a cowboy to flirt with, a one-night stand, maybe. Company for her trip, but she had no intentions of conducting a long-distance relationship with a cowboy in North Dakota from New York City.

For all he knew, she had a boyfriend back home.

He certainly wasn't interested in someone like that.

But Carna, on the other hand...

Still, to walk into the stables after thinking about her constantly for the last three days, deciding that maybe there was a chance for them after all, and to hear her express surprise, disbelief, disgust even, when Abrielle had suggested that there might be more between them, had thrown cold water over everything that he'd been thinking.

He hadn't been angry, he'd been hurt. But it was easier to be mad than to be hurt, so that's the way he acted.

After he'd taken a shower, he'd taken his time with the horses, only speaking to Carna when he absolutely had to. Which wasn't much.

She'd gone down the list of everything that she'd done, and Zeke had been there, listening to everything that happened, taking notes about what Miller wanted done, and assuring them that he would take good care of the horses while they were gone.

Now, he was just stalling. Pretending that he needed to check on Fancy's foal, but he really didn't. She was fine. Three more days and he'd be back home working with her again. He didn't need to spend any extra time with her now.

Of course, he was also annoyed with Pepper. Apparently, Pepper had taken to following Carna around everywhere. Now, Pepper was back on his heels, but he cast sad, puppy dog eyes back, like he somehow wanted Miller to spend more time with Carna, so he could be with the two people he loved most in the world, instead of just the one.

If Miller hadn't walked in to hear Abrielle and Carna talking, he probably would have thought it was cute. A sign even.

But now? It just made him mad. His dog couldn't even be faithful to him. He had to get sucked into Carna's charm.

And now, he had a four-hour drive and three days to spend with her.

He wasn't looking forward to it.

Except that wasn't true. Because he really was. As angry...hurt as he was, he did want to spend time with her. And that annoyed him.

He heard the crunch of gravel before a person stepped into his peripheral vision.

He didn't have to look to know it was Carna. He could smell her. Not in a bad way, there was some kind of fresh, familiar scent that followed her.

He couldn't even put a name on it, but it reminded him of rain and the way the ground smelled afterward. It wasn't a bad smell, it made him feel...comfortable.

He gritted his jaw and turned.

"You ready to go?" His words were short, and he didn't try to modulate them.

"I was coming out to ask you the same question."

"Yeah... I'm tired, and I can't wait to get there."

She jerked her head up and didn't say anything as he started striding toward the stable. As far as he knew, all they had to do was put the cooler in the back of the truck, and he had to run upstairs and grab his bag.

He hadn't had time to wash clothes, so he could only hope he'd be able to find a laundromat and have time to wash them before tomorrow morning.

"Your stuff is in the dryer," Carna said from behind him.

"My stuff?"

"I threw your clothes in the washer as soon as you got home, they're ready."

"Okay," he said, not sure what else to say. Probably thank you, except he didn't want to. Didn't want to owe her anything.

"You mean you touched my stuff?" he asked, and it sounded more like a snarl.

"I wasn't sure how many clothes you had. I know I don't have enough to be gone for three days, wear something, and then to be gone for three more days. Maybe you do."

He didn't. Especially since he hadn't washed clothes for two days before he left, since he didn't know he was going on a crop-dusting run.

"They're in the dryer?"

"Yeah. It's doing its cooldown things right now."

Her words were calm, she wasn't flirting, and she wasn't smiling. Just talking to him matter-of-factly. That probably helped more than anything. It diffused his anger.

"Sorry you're stuck with me." He didn't need to say that, but the words slipped out as he started striding toward the apartments.

"I don't feel like I'm stuck with you," she said, keeping up with his stride, her dog at her heels.

Pepper followed him, too, tail wagging, probably in all of his glory now that his favorite people in the world worked together again.

The traitor.

"That's not what I heard. But it doesn't matter. Are you taking the dogs over to the house so the kids can watch them until we leave?" He didn't want to talk about "them." Shouldn't have allowed those words to come out of his mouth, but he supposed he'd been thinking about it and it slipped.

He'd have to do better.

"Sure. I'll give you a hand with the cooler when I get back. It has drinks, stuff for the trip, and sandwiches for tonight. After that, we're on our own for food, although the water should last us the whole time. It's heavy."

He jerked his head but had no intention of allowing her to help. He'd have his bag on the back of the truck along with cooler when she got back from the house. He'd make sure of it.

He was closing the tailgate when she came walking back.

"I told you I'd help you with that," she said as she got nearer.

"I didn't need it," he said, glancing at her. "Ready?"

She jerked her chin and went to the passenger side of the pickup, climbing in and buckling her belt.

They didn't say anything for a while, and he thought it might be a pretty quiet ride. There weren't a whole lot of turns until he hit Montana. And so he settled down, trying to think of anything but the next three days and how he was going to have to try to continue to ignore the woman beside him.

"She surprised me. That's why I sounded so shocked. Not because I thought the idea was repugnant."

He hadn't expected her to address it so directly. But he appreciated it. They could put it to rest fast. "I do, so there's that."

"She didn't seem to think you did."

"She's wrong."

"She said Smith told her that after talking to you, he knew the idea was not repugnant to you, either."

He didn't say anything. He'd already lied, if he was being perfectly honest with himself. Just because he wanted it to be true didn't mean it was. "Smith has a big mouth."

"I suppose that Abrielle could have gone to you and said the same thing. I... She had me admitting that you were different than what I expected. Different than what you used to be. That you were someone I admire." She blew out a breath. "What I can't figure out is whether she was trying to do that to make us be a couple which would be more interesting at the competition, or whether she was doing it for our benefit. I want to think the second, because I think she likes us and wants the best for us. But I'm not entirely sure."

"If Abrielle said it, it was for our good. She would never put winning a contest ahead of our welfare."

"Even when the future of the ranch hinges on it?"

"Even then."

She was quiet for a bit.

"Now you decide you don't want to talk?"

"You just defended Abrielle so confidently. Like you know her so well. And yet, you were so eager to jump on believing the worst of me. It...made me feel bad."

Okay. She had a point there. He supposed if she were going on about some other guy, even if it was Smith, her brother, while she held him in derision, he wouldn't like that either. Except, instead of saying she hurt him and made him feel bad, he would act angry.

"I guess... I guess we need to figure some things out. I'm sorry. I definitely don't like Abrielle more than I like you, if that's what you were saying."

"That's just how it felt."

"Maybe she's safer. It's safer for me to say that I know what she's thinking and I have confidence in her. It feels a little bit dangerous for me to say that about you, since I'm not sure how you feel about me, and I feel like I'm sticking my neck out and possibly risking getting my head chopped off."

"I haven't chopped anyone's head off for years. In fact, I'm not even sure where my knife is."

"There's this new invention called the guillotine..."

"You are hilarious. And so up with the times."

"Hey, it's quick and easy, from what I hear anyway. I guess I haven't talked to anyone who's actually experienced it."

"Right. None of my victims have sur-
vived. Sorry."

He grinned, looking across the seat at
her. "So I would be the first?" He supposed he was teasing her just a little bit,
but he couldn't seem to help it.

"You're making an awful big assump-
tion there," she said, rather softly, back
at him.

That made his grin widen. "I'm pretty
confident I know what the outcome is
going to be."

"All right. You continue to be confident." She lifted her brows, then looked
forward, a smug look on her face.

His hands tightened on the wheel. He
knew what he needed to do. He'd been
a jerk. Again. Maybe not quite as bad as

last time, but she hadn't done anything to deserve his sour mood.

"I'm sorry I was short with you."

"I'm starting to get used to it."

"Oh, that's not even funny."

"I know. The problem is, you keep being the first person to apologize, and that makes me feel bad. I should be the one to say I'm sorry first. Next time, I'm going to beat you to it. You're forgiven, by the way. And I'm sorry."

"I was the one who wasn't kind. You don't have anything to apologize for."

"I could have been nicer. And I knew exactly what the problem was. You heard what I said, and I should have apologized right then. I should have let you know that it wasn't what you thought."

"Wasn't it?"

"No. I told you, I was just surprised. Surely that would surprise you as well?"

"I don't know. I've spent a lot of time these last three days thinking about things I didn't think I would be thinking about ever. It's been a little bit weird."

"I sure hope you were paying attention to the job you were doing."

"Yeah. Flying a plane does take a bit of concentration. But there's a lot of downtime too. Deliberate downtime," he added with a smirk.

She laughed, and he enjoyed the sound.

"So another truce?" she finally said.

"Is that what it is?"

"We could agree to be friends?" She looked across the seat, lifting her brows in question.

He glanced at her face, reading nothing there but maybe a little bit of hope. Definitely not distaste or disgust. "I think I'd like that. In fact, I know I would."

"Then let's do that. We're friends. And maybe we'll get to be good friends by the end of the competition. Which, by the way, I'm rather nervous about. After all, you know I've only ridden a horse once in my life before. What if..."

"I think saying 'what if' is a really bad way to live your life. You need to have statements that give you confidence. Kind of like..."

"Like what?"

"Like, God has us here for a reason. I'm not sure what that is, but I'll do my best. And assume that whatever it is that He wants me to do, He's going to accomplish His purpose even in my weakness."

"Oh, that's a good one. Ouch."

"Hey. I wasn't hitting you, I was helping. There's a difference now that we're friends." He grinned at her.

"Right. Helping. You're helping me. That wasn't supposed to hurt." She rubbed her shoulder, like he punched her.

"Okay, that's not gonna happen."

"I know." She pulled in a breath and blew it out. "You're right. I'm here, God knows it, and He's not going to have me doing anything that...that He doesn't want me to do. Even if it's something that I can't do. Like...roping a cow."

"Typically, we rope steers, but yeah, whatever."

"That's kind of splitting hairs for someone who's never done it."

"Not going to disagree about that. But there's no point in borrowing trouble; you're going to agree with that, right?"

"Right. No borrowing trouble. I'm going to believe that however big of a fool I make out of myself, God has a purpose for it."

"There might be someone who needs to see you fail in order to feel like they are not a failure. Or it might be because you need to fail in order to grow. You know? To be humble, to grow in being humble, to get rid of your pride, or just to realize that failure isn't everything, or maybe sometimes you fail and it makes you more determined to succeed. Whatever it is, God has a lesson. You just have to be willing to learn it."

"And that takes being humble. Since I know that I'm going into this thing doing things that I'm not comfortable with at all."

"Exactly. God has to take us out of our comfort zone, and that works to grow us. That's uncomfortable, but it helps us be better people. As crazy as that sounds."

"You're right." She took another breath and then laughed a little. "I'm still nervous, but I know you're right. There's a purpose, there is an opportunity for growth, lessons to be learned, and maybe I'll never even know the people who needed to see me make a fool out of myself."

Miller really appreciated the fact that she was able to calm herself down and realize that the important thing was what the Lord wanted and not what they wanted.

Sometimes he had a hard time with that. He wanted to reach out and get his way so badly that he could hardly talk himself into just realizing that he needed to allow God to work.

"So, have you ever participated in something like this before?"

They chatted for the rest of the drive, easy conversation, with comfortable silences at times.

He felt like he was talking to an old friend, even though Carna was basically a new friend. Even if she was an old acquaintance.

They made it to the hotel, where the ranch had reserved two rooms.

After getting parked, they ate some of the sandwiches she'd packed and took a couple of drinks to their rooms which were side by side but not adjoining.

"If you need anything during the night, you can let me know."

"Thanks. I probably won't bother you unless it's an extreme emergency. I've

got water, and I can't imagine that anything else will crop up."

"All right, I just don't want you to hes-
itate, out of some weird idea that you
might be bothering me or something."

"You've been away for the last three
days. I'm sure you're pretty tired."

"Tired and wanting to sleep in my own
bed, but this will do." He liked that she'd
be close. But he didn't say that. It was
much more comfortable to have her
there than it was to be sleeping in a bed
hundreds of miles away from her.

He wasn't sure quite when that happened, and it was a little bit scary, although less scary now than it had been,
since he was at least sure they were
friends.

They set a time to meet the next morning so they could eat breakfast before they went to the competition. Competitors had to be there by eleven, with the competition starting at noon.

He waited until she used her card to get in the door, then watched as she disappeared, listening for the deadbolt chain to go across the door.

That was all he could do to make sure that she was safe.

It hardly felt like enough.

And despite how the day had started, he found himself really looking forward to the next day and the start of the competition.

Chapter 26

"This is interesting," Carna said as she looked at the schedule in front of her.

"I'll say. It's the most interesting cowboy competition I've ever heard of," Miller said, although he didn't seem terribly upset.

That was a relief to Carna, because while some of the items on the list were things she expected, like Muck the Mess and Stack the Stuff, which she as-sumed was probably stacking hay bales, there were ones that she wouldn't have guessed in a million years that they would have to do.

She looked at the list again. Several competitions stuck out to her.

Dance with Your Dude.

Pickup Your Partner. What in the world was that anyway?

Time for Tea.

What could they possibly want them to do that had to do with tea?

But the one that really had her concerned was the last one on the list.

Kiss Your Partner.

Really? Not that she hadn't had thoughts about kissing Miller. She would be lying if she said she hadn't, but...for the competition? That was definitely not something she wanted to do.

It was almost funny now, the way Miller had given her a pep talk yesterday in the truck about God's will.

She wasn't quite sure whether kissing her partner was really something that God would move her the whole way from New Hampshire to do.

Regardless, that was not on the schedule for today.

The competitions were going to be live streamed, but there was still a big crowd mingling around out in the bleacher area.

They were out in the middle of some barns and fields that were used for the county fair with a big arena off to the side.

There were lots of food stands, music, and she'd even heard that there was going to be a demolition derby tonight, so while the competition was the main draw, it wasn't the only draw.

They sat through a meeting with the rules, where they had been told that the judges' scores were final, that anyone caught cheating would be disqualified immediately, and that they could not switch partners once the competition started, so if someone got hurt, they were both out.

Nothing surprising there. But at the end of that meeting, they'd been handed the sheet with all of the names of the competitions on it, and that's where Carna had really gotten thrown for a loop.

"All right, if there aren't any questions, we'll go ahead and mosey on over to the first shed. That's where the hay bales are, and that's where we'll start with our first competition, which is Stack the Stuff. Things might be a little different, since we went out of our way to make this competition unique and hopefully very entertaining." The man in charge, speaking into a microphone that sounded tinny coming through the speakers, grinned at the competitors from under his big cowboy hat.

He wore the traditional western garb with a button-down plaid shirt, complete with fringes that waved in the breeze, a big buckle on his jeans, and fancy cowboy boots.

It made Carna feel a little under-dressed, even though she was wearing pretty much the same thing, just not quite as fancy.

Regardless, he led them over to a shed, the whole front of which was open.

There were five bays, and outside of each bay, about twenty feet away, was a bunch of hay bales.

"The object is to get the hay bales into the shed and stack them."

Carna waited, but those were the only instructions they were given. He didn't say how high or exactly how they wanted them stacked.

She assumed, since the instructions didn't say, that was open for interpretation.

She and Miller whispered about it while the man worked the crowd, talking about the competitors and giving details and behind-the-scenes stories.

She couldn't believe how many people had come to watch, nor how excited people seemed to be about it. Moms and dads sat with their kids, laughing and pointing as the announcer talked about the contestants.

"I'll go over, throw the bales to you, and you can stack them."

"Sounds good. I'm a little bit relieved to find out that we're actually going to do something I know how to do."

He smiled at her, a reassuring smile that told her that it didn't matter how she did, he was going to be okay with it.

After talking to Abrielle, she knew the ranch did not expect them to work miracles. Just to do their best. To think less about winning and more about charming the people by just being themselves. She would do what she could and let the results be what they would be.

"All right, contestants, stand in your bay until the whistle blows. First couple with your hay all stacked is the winner. Don't forget, keep working until you're finished, because you get points for your placements."

Carna's stomach twirled, but she looked at Miller and gave him what she hoped was a reassuring smile which he returned.

The announcer blew his whistle, and Miller ran to the hay.

He was able to throw the bales so they hit and rolled toward the back of the shed.

She grabbed the first one and finished carrying it the rest of the way to the back, figuring that it looked like there were about thirty bales, so if she stacked them five long, three wide, and two high, they'd fit nicely. She could do a little bit higher, but if she tried to stack them much more than two, she would slow herself down in a big way.

Her calculations were completely accurate—she'd guessed at the number of hay bales and stacked them for years—and they were well ahead of the other contestants when, on the second-to-last bale, Miller threw it and one of the strings broke. Hay flew everywhere.

"I'll get it," Miller called as he ran to pick up the last bale and threw it over all the hay that had scattered.

She stacked the last one he threw and then went to help gather the pats of hay. She held the bale together while Miller tied the broken string around the bale, cutting the good string and using it, too.

It was what she would do if she had broken the bale while putting them up in the haymow if they didn't throw it directly down and feed it immediately to the cows.

It seemed like both of them had done it a time or two before, and they worked well together.

They laughed when Carna got her hand caught in the twine and pulled it out quickly so Miller was still able to tighten the knot. She picked up the pat they couldn't fit back in the bale, while he carried the makeshift bale and stuck it in the last row. She put the loose pat on top.

Still, it took some time to get it together, and in that amount of time, three of the five contestants passed them and finished.

They still beat the last couple, which was no small feat, considering the trouble they'd had.

Still, Carna was disappointed, because this was one competition where she knew she would be able to do a good job. It didn't involve riding horses, or roping anything, or any of the other things she knew she wouldn't be any good at.

Still, they laughed and had a good time, and the crowd seemed to be rooting for them. Maybe it was just her imagination, because as far as she knew, they didn't know anyone here. No one from the dude ranch had come, because it was just too busy this time of year to spare anyone.

The announcer congratulated the winner, and they moved off as the hay bales were taken back down and set out for the next group of five since there were twenty couples altogether.

The crowd hollered at them as they passed, some of them telling them they got a rough break, but they did a good job anyway.

"Hey, cowboy? Here's my number!" one contestant yelled, throwing a piece of paper in Miller's direction.

He didn't make any attempt to catch it, didn't even look to see where it landed.

"I'm getting the idea that this is less about doing things well and more about getting people excited about who we are and our personalities, if that makes sense," Carna said as they followed the contestants to the waiting area.

"I had the same idea," Miller said under his breath. "The winner does get a lot of attention, but they're trying to put on a show for the crowd. It wouldn't surprise me at all if they loosened that string on purpose, just to see the hay fly apart and to see how we handled it. To give us a chance to chum up to the viewers."

"I never thought that they might have done it on purpose. You really think so?"

"I think it's a possibility anyway," Miller said, shrugging his shoulders.

Carna thought he really might be onto something, when after sitting in the contestant area for fifteen minutes, they moved out to the Time for Tea competition.

To Carna's surprise, it was an iced tea making competition.

"Are they serious?" Carna whispered to Miller as the judge in charge explained that each of them were going to be given access to the kitchen and twenty minutes to make a gallon of iced tea. The crowd would be the judges. As they all got a taste, they were to mark their preferences on their scorecard.

Carna discovered contestants were at a disadvantage because they had no idea what the scorecard was asking about the tea.

"I feel like we're working with blinders on," Miller murmured when it was their turn to walk to the kitchen.

"Not knowing what everyone's expecting?" Carna asked, looking up at him and directing her words to his ear, low enough that they couldn't be heard, as they continued to walk in front of the crowd, toward the counter.

The "kitchen" was set up on a stage, with a counter and cupboards, a refrigerator and freezer.

It was restocked after each contestant made their tea.

Miller and she were the fourth couple to do tea, since they took them in order of the places they'd earned in the hay-stacking contest.

"This is not what I expected out of a cowboy competition."

"Me, either. But they said they wanted to be unique, and this is definitely unique."

"After they set the timer, I'm going to check the freezer. If they have any lemonade concentrate in there, let's use some of that. My grandma used to do that with her tea, and I thought it made it really good."

"That's a great idea. That would be a little bit different than what everyone else is doing."

"Yeah. That could be an advantage."

They nodded to each other and then were quiet for a bit as the announcer talked about them, mentioned Sweet Briar Ranch in North Dakota, and explained that they had a little bit of trouble on the hay-stacking contest.

Carna tried to think of anything else that would be helpful for the tea, and by the time the announcer had told them to start the contest, she had a couple of other ideas brewing in her head.

It surprised her, although she supposed it probably shouldn't have, that she and Miller worked so well together.

She seemed to be the one who went out on a limb, while he was the steady one behind her. She appreciated that and hoped he felt they were as compatible as what she did.

Regardless, she found the lemonade concentrate in the freezer, which surprised her, but she didn't take the time to celebrate, just walked back to where he had filled their pitcher one third full with water and put a cup of sugar in it.

"Gram always used one third of the can. Does that work for you?"

"I say we follow her recipe. It seemed to have made an impression on you," he said, and he winked at her.

The announcer noticed that right away, and the crowd tittered as he said that he thought he saw the cowboy wink.

Maybe Miller was a little bit taciturn and quiet at times, but he was not shy. He called out, "You didn't just think it, it happened." Then, he gave a great big grin, looked at Carna, and lowered one eyelid slowly, so there was no doubt about the wink that time.

The crowd roared and clapped.

They were able to finish making the tea, filling the pitcher up the rest of the way with ice cubes, since the water was so warm. In order to come in under time, they didn't have time to allow the water to cool after they boiled it and put the tea bags in.

"All right, everyone gets a small taste, and we'll see if the secret ingredient that the Sweet Briar couple used made a difference."

They walked off the stage as two helpers walked around, giving everyone a cup and pouring a little bit of tea into it.

The announcer was droning on about scorecards as they left and were directed to the large arena.

That was what Carna had been dreading, and while she was pretty confident in their tea, she cast an apologetic glance at Miller. "I know I'm going to be the weak link in this."

"Don't worry about it. I told you, I don't think it's how well we do, I think it's how well the crowd likes us just being ourselves."

She took a deep breath, then nodded. Okay, she couldn't rope, she couldn't ride, and she couldn't do most of the things these Westerners did on their ranches. But she could pull out her charming smile, her goofy self, and see if she couldn't complement Miller as he did everything perfectly.

That was what she attempted for the rest of the afternoon as they did three different competitions in the arena involving horses, ropes, and cattle.

The cattle, Carna was confident around, the horses and ropes, not so much.

But she did her best, trying to be game and fun, to complement Miller and allow him to do what he did best.

Miller played along, and while she took several spills and ended up dirty from head to toe, to her surprise she had fun anyway, and finally they were leaving the arena after the calf-roping competition, where she threw the rope, totally missed the calf, and managed to fall off her horse at the same time, and Miller, who had gone just before her, galloped out on his horse, stopped beside her, and gave her a hand up.

The crowd had roared at that, and Miller had eaten it up, lifting his hat, waving it.

Carna tried to pay attention, but she was a little distracted by her arms around Miller's waist.

She had no idea what it felt like when they were in high school, but she had an idea that it wasn't quite that hard.

Regardless, in high school she hadn't had any desire to take a hold of it, but now, she didn't want to let go. Not even to wave.

Or to get off, after he stopped the horse when they made it out of the arena and back behind the chutes.

"Need me to find a mounting block? Or a fence?"

"No. I can slide off. I guess I was just enjoying the feeling of being safe."

"And finished. Since that was the last thing on our list for today."

"Yes. Finished. I think I'm going to take a bath tonight and soak in some hot water. I've got a feeling my muscles are going to make themselves felt in a big way tomorrow."

Instead of laughing, he froze.

She could feel his breath stop under her hands. She was about to ask him what the problem was, when he said, "I suppose you need someone to give you a massage."

There was a husky note in his voice, one that hadn't been there before.

She hadn't realized how her words might have been construed, and she hadn't meant that at all, except...he didn't seem upset by the idea.

Suddenly her mouth was dry, and she tried to swallow. Her throat was tight.

"I suppose," she managed to croak out.

"I'd hate to do poorly tomorrow because you're sore," he said slowly.

"Me too." She wasn't exactly sure what she was saying. She had absolutely zero intention of allowing anyone to give her a massage. Except the idea of Miller rubbing her back wasn't exactly unwelcome.

Before he could say anything else, she said, "All right. I'm going to slide off. Hopefully I don't land on my butt."

"You've done that often enough today. I would say that you're practiced up, but I wouldn't want to make you feel bad."

"I know. And you didn't fall once. It's hardly fair."

"Oh, trust me. I've fallen plenty of times. Everyone does when they're learning."

"I would say you probably did it when you were a kid, but I knew you when you were a kid, and you weren't doing this kind of thing. So, I guess you were an adult too, just an adult without an audience."

"It's the audience that makes all the difference, isn't it?" he said, and all traces of the husky note were gone. Almost as though he'd taken her lead and allowed her to change the subject. Allowed her to lead them away from whatever it was that they were going toward the last time they were talking.

She managed to get her leg over the horse, but it involved holding on tighter to his waist, pressing her head against his back while she slowly lowered herself to the ground.

Her feet and legs were a bit numb, and she stumbled, but he grabbed a hold of her, putting his hand on her shoulder, while his horse stood completely still.

"This is a well-trained horse," he said, and she laughed a little.

"That's to my benefit, I'm sure, since all he needed to do was breathe and it would have knocked me over there."

"But you're good."

"Yeah. I'm sorry you had to babysit me."

"I'm telling you, it's okay. I think we're doing pretty good. At least we're doing what we set out to do, which was to bring attention to the ranch. They're talking about the Sweet Briar dude ranch, and maybe I'm being a little bit egotistical, but I think we're a crowd favorite. And that's partly due to the fact that you've fallen down so many times, and you've gotten up every time and kept on. People admire that kind of spirit in someone. I admire that kind of spirit. In you."

He swung a leg over the saddle and dropped to the ground.

An attendant came and took the horse, leading it away, and she was left standing alone with Miller.

"Thanks."

She could go on about what she admired in him. Because she did. He'd learned a lot in the amount of time since he'd started ranching. Stuff that other people had been doing all their lives, stuff he just started doing and was really good at.

But not just that, the way he'd encouraged her, helped her, and decided that if they weren't going to win the competition, they could at least do what they'd come for. She loved the way his mind had shifted, and he'd gone from wanting to win, to...allowing God to use their weakness and turn it into a strength.

She wasn't quite sure she'd ever seen someone live out that teaching quite like this before, but she appreciated his leading and his example, because he was right. Their weakness really was their strength.

Chapter 27

The second day of the competition was even worse than the first. Carna spent more time off her horse than on it. She must have fallen a dozen or more times, so many times that she lost count.

Almost everything was supposed to be done from the back of a horse, and her riding skills, not to mention her balance and instincts, were almost nonexistent.

"I feel so bad for my horse," she said after one particularly bad fall, one she highly suspected was caused by her horse totally not understanding what she wanted it to do.

"I feel bad for you, and I'm getting sick and tired of seeing you on the ground. I'm kicking myself for letting Smith talk me into going on that crop-dusting run. I wish I could have stayed home and worked with you on riding." Miller shook his head. "Actually, what I really wish is that I would have just stayed home, no matter what Smith said."

Carna shook her head. She knew he didn't mean it. "The ranch needed the crop-dusting money. That's part of what we do to support it. It doesn't pay to stay home and teach me to ride. Plus, I actually think it pays better to have me on the ground so much. We're in dead last place, but we're definitely the crowd favorite."

She wasn't sure whether she talked him out of anything or not, but he couldn't disagree with her. There was a definite difference in sound decibels anytime they came out to compete.

The crowd groaned as one every time she fell off her horse, and they cheered even louder every time she got back up off the ground.

"I have to say, I'm pretty sure I'm going to be black and blue in places I've never been black and blue before. In fact, I think it's going to be kind of hard to find anywhere that I'm not black and blue. I even hit my face twice."

"Your one eye is a little swollen," Miller said, his eyes roving over her face like he was trying to find anything else that was wrong with her.

There was no hint of a smile on his face; he actually looked rather angry.

"Listen, if this does what it's supposed to do for the ranch, that's all we need, right?" She was trying to placate him, but if anything, his jaw tightened even more.

"I don't think it's worth it. You haven't been seriously hurt, but you could have been, and there's still time for that. It just takes landing the wrong way one time, or your horse not being able to stop and putting his hoof down in exactly the wrong spot."

He opened his mouth to say more, but nothing else came out.

"I think you're worried about me," she said, bumping his shoulder with hers, as the announcer called their names.

"Somebody has to. You act like you're having a good time. You can't possibly be enjoying this."

"I have to say, I don't care if I ever see another horse again."

"Don't let this sour you on horses." He wasn't begging, but he did sound a little bit concerned, like she was being serious and really wouldn't want to ever ride again.

"I love horses. I just... I'm not sure how badly I want to get back on one, once I don't have to anymore. I think I will be very happy taking care of them from the ground."

They didn't have a chance to talk any-more, because it was their turn to go out in the arena.

Thankfully, that was the last competi-tion for the day, and while Carna once again fell off her horse, three times to be exact, and they didn't move up in the standings at all, they definitely still had the sympathy of the crowd.

After they were finished, and the atten-dants had come and taken their horses, Miller put his arm around her shoulders, and they walked toward his pickup to-gether.

"I'd ask if you want to go out to eat, but I'm guessing that probably the only thing you want to do is fill up a tub of hot water and sit in it for a really long time."

"I'm not the slightest bit hungry." She lifted her shoulders. That was the truth. She really did hurt all over and ached every time she took a step. Eating was the very last thing she had on her mind.

But she didn't want to complain. She had a feeling that if she started saying how badly she actually hurt, Miller would pull out of the competition. She didn't want that. She didn't want all of her previous suffering to be for nothing. If they were going to get guests out to Sweet Briar, if they were going to save the ranch, she would keep going until they had reached the end.

"I'm just bummed that there's no chance for us to win."

"Normally, I would give myself a little pep talk, thinking that we can have a great comeback, but... I think you're right. There's no chance for us to win." He did grin at her a little, and she returned it.

"Regardless, whatever we do tomorrow, we're going to celebrate when the competition is over. Is that a deal?"

She lifted her brows at him, and he looked down. "Do you think you're going to feel better tomorrow than you do today?"

"Surely we had all the horse competition today. Surely whatever they're going to have us do tomorrow isn't going to involve me on the ground pretty much all the time when I'm supposed to be on a horse."

"I don't know. The first day wasn't too bad, so maybe we'll have some more contests like that." He didn't sound like he was convinced of it, and neither was she. But in order for her to be able to look forward to the next day, she had to tell herself that it was going to get better. She couldn't think that it wasn't, or she was going to have a hard time getting herself up in the morning.

Actually, it was hard enough to get herself up the next morning as her alarm went off.

It was Saturday, and the competition started at nine o'clock. They had to be there at eight, and she set her alarm for seven thirty.

Normally she was up long before that, but she slept like a log the night before after taking three pain pills.

They wore off sometime during the night, because when she rolled over, it was all she could do not to groan.

Somehow she got out of bed, swallowed three more pills, since they didn't kill her the night before, and managed to get dressed.

She told herself that she would be home, sleeping in her own bed, by nightfall. That was inspiring, and she even told herself that she could take the next day off. Then she told herself she was being a baby and a person could work with sore muscles. It wasn't that big of a deal.

"You look terrible," is what Miller greeted her with.

"Thanks. You actually look...really good." It was the pain pills talking. She couldn't think of anything else to say, and the truth just slipped out.

"I don't think you meant to say that," he accused.

"You're right. I'm blaming the meds."

"I think you should take those meds every day. They help with your eyesight."

"I think I'm going to be taking them for a while, so you'll get your wish. But they're starting to take the edge off, so I'm feeling like we're ready to go."

"Are you sure?"

"I sure am. After all, if we're going to lose, we're going to lose in style, right?"

"I don't think I've ever come in dead last in anything that I've ever entered before in my life," he said with a little grin, and she knew he was teasing her.

She supposed that was probably what he had been doing back when they were younger. Teasing her, and she just took it the wrong way and then said something rude back to him, and they turned out to be antagonistic toward each other, when neither one of them really meant it that way.

After all, he wasn't accusing her of being the reason that they were losing. And there hadn't been anyone more concerned about her yesterday than he was. In fact, if it hadn't been for her talking him into it, they probably would have quit halfway through the day.

"So I decided something last night," he started as they got in the pickup, and he backed out of the hotel lot.

"Okay."

"If we're doing horse stuff today, you and I are pulling out of the competition and we're going home."

"No!" His words upset her, and she hadn't quite gotten to the point where she could form coherent sentences, but she knew no was the right answer.

"I don't recall asking. I just informed you what we are going to do. And before you get all upset," he put a hand up, "I know, it sounded high-handed, but if you were me, you'd be doing the same thing. And I know it. So don't argue with me. You wouldn't be able to be partnered with anyone, whether it was me or someone else, and watch them get beat up the whole time you're competing. Ranch or no ranch."

She couldn't argue with that. He was right.

"All right. I still disagree. I want to stay. I want to finish. But I can't say that you're wrong. If it were my partner having all the trouble, I would be saying the same thing that you're saying right now."

"I thought so. I wish I would've done it yesterday. I mean, if we take zeros, whether we compete or whether we don't compete, it doesn't really matter?"

"It does. The crowd wouldn't have been on our side the way they were. We wouldn't have had so many people seeing us and rooting for us. In fact, I don't know if it's true or not, but a couple of times, I thought I heard people talking about us being on social media. I... I have to admit my head hurt so bad yesterday that I didn't even try to look on any of my accounts. Someone said we were trending, and I heard the word 'viral' going around."

"I wasn't sore, my head didn't hurt, but I'm not on social media, so I really don't know."

It didn't take long to get to the fairgrounds, where the parking lot was already filling up. They parked, and Carna tried not to wince as they got out of the truck.

She had thrown a couple more pills in her pocket, and they had been very good at handing out water whenever they needed it, so she knew she'd be good for the rest of the day, although the competition was supposed to end by three.

They were among the last competitors to arrive, and they didn't have long to wait for the leader with the megaphone to get up in front of them.

"We have a great lineup today, and the crowd is already anticipating what we're going to be doing."

It had taken Carna a little bit of time to figure it out, but they divided the twenty competitors into groups of five, and they were all doing different competitions. So another group of five was doing some of the competitions that they had done yesterday. She didn't exactly understand how it was all divided up, but it really wasn't up to her to understand, she just had to do her best.

The megaphone guy in front of them was the leader of their group, giving them the instructions each time they needed it.

"Today we are going to start with a cooking competition—king ranch chicken. A dish that every Westerner knows how to make, and we're going to see who can do it the best. If we start out now, your meals will be ready for the crowd to start sampling by eleven. So, follow me, we're heading to the kitchen."

"I'm pretty sure I'm not going to be falling off any horses from now until eleven anyway," Carna said as they moseyed on behind the man with the megaphone.

"That's good news to me. Not to mention, king ranch chicken is one of my favorites. I think we're going to do pretty well on this."

"Have you made it before?"

"Nope. I do believe this is the area where you're supposed to shine."

"Cooking is, um, not really my thing." It didn't seem like she had a thing. She tried not to let that get her discouraged and down. After all, she had been thinking yesterday if they could just get her off the horse, she could do pretty well.

What was she good at?

Getting back up.

She shook her head, still wishing she had a talent, but she supposed that getting up was a talent in itself.

They were taken to a kitchen where there were five stations set up with various ingredients for the king ranch chicken.

"I don't have a recipe for you to follow, but I've got ingredients sitting out. You can use whatever you want, as much as you want, to fill up the dish in front of you."

They looked at the dish, and Carna tried to figure out how much chicken it would take to fill it.

"If you want, you can look up recipes online or come up with your own. Totally up to you." The man held up his hands. "We're interested in taste and the end result. We don't care how you get there."

"Well, that'll make it a lot easier. We can watch a YouTube video," Carna said, trying to ignore the ache in her neck as she looked up at Miller. She was feeling a lot better than she had been. The pills had taken most of the pain away, and as her body got loosened up, her muscles moved easier.

Miller already had his phone out and was googling king ranch chicken while the megaphone dude talked to the crowd who had gathered in the stands.

She let Miller go, figuring that he'd pick out a recipe for them.

"All right, folks. You have thirty minutes to put it together, then it's going in the oven," megaphone man said, then he hollered into the megaphone, "Go!"

"How about this recipe?" Miller said, almost immediately.

Carna looked over his shoulder, saw the picture of the end result, and said, "Looks good to me."

She had no idea, because cooking really wasn't her thing. But she could follow a recipe, surely.

"All right. It says we need to chop up some onions and peppers and sauté them in a pan. I'm not sure what sauté means, but it looks like they're putting a pan on the stove and it has some oil in it. So I assume it means fry."

"All right. I know how to chop onions and peppers, so I can do that much."

She did that while he looked on down the recipe and started opening cans of condensed soup and diced tomatoes. She thought she saw him put some broth and sour cream in as well, which really made it look delicious.

She didn't even ask about the spices, just was happy that he was throwing it all together, and she didn't stop to clap when he pulled some cheese out as well.

"All right. I think these things are soft. We don't want them brown, do we?" she asked a little bit later as she'd gotten the peppers and onions chopped and in the skillet, cooking them until they were soft and translucent.

"That looks perfect. Just like the picture." He held up his phone, looking at what was on the recipe versus what was in the pan. "All right, I think you put that in here, and we'll stir it all up."

She did that. Then, since he had all the rest of the ingredients ready, they did the layering like the recipe said and were done ten minutes before the bell rang.

"I'm feeling pretty confident about that," Miller said. He laughed. "Neither one of us fell down, there was no blood, even though I let you use the knife, which, in hindsight, probably wasn't my smartest move, and I think if the crowd has any idea that they're tasting ours, they'll vote for us, just because they feel bad for you."

"So you think we'll win by such a large margin that we might not come in last anymore?" She laughed, knowing that that was impossible. They were so far last that even if they won every competition that day by a mile, it wouldn't be enough to get them even into nineteenth position instead of twentieth.

Not that she minded, because he was right, the crowd was definitely on their side.

They waited for the rest of the contestants to be done, and by then, Carna was feeling pretty good.

"All right, folks, we have two contests left."

Just two more contests to get through. Carna did not sigh in relief, but she felt like it.

After all, the cooking contest was fun. The horse contests the day before had been fun as well, even if she had landed on the ground most of the time. It had just been fun to work with Miller.

Their leader led them out onto a stage, where a crowd of people sat in chairs facing it, in the back was standing room only, and people were poking their heads in from the sides.

The place was packed, and Carna didn't even know what they were doing for the contest yet.

The announcer picked up a microphone and spoke into it. "Welcome to the dancing contest, ladies and gentlemen."

A dancing contest.

"Are you up to this?" Miller leaned down and spoke softly in her ear.

She nodded immediately. "Yep. I'm down."

It didn't matter how much it hurt, she could do a dancing contest. "Actually, normally I would say that I might be a little bit self-conscious to dance in front of people, but after falling on my butt a million times yesterday, I really don't think I can make myself look any worse." She lifted her shoulder and gave a crooked smile. "It was kinda freeing."

"For you," Miller said, with a hint of a smile on his face, which told her that he was going to do whatever needed to be done, but he probably wasn't looking forward to it.

"All right, contestants, we have a medley of music for you, do your best. For the next five minutes, the spotlight is on the five of you." He pointed toward the side of the stage. "Sound people, do your thing."

Carna assumed that meant the contest was beginning, and sure enough, the music began right after that. An upbeat piece with a driving beat pumped out of the speakers.

Carna met Miller's eyes. She gave a little shrug of her shoulders, and then she started to dance.

She probably looked ridiculous, but she felt like the best dancing was probably dancing where one didn't care how one looked.

She kept an eye on Miller and tried to stay with him, and he seemed to do the same with her. Considering it was the first time they'd ever danced together, she supposed they didn't do too bad. At least, she didn't step on his toes once, and she didn't fall down.

And she considered both of those things wins.

The music surged into something else, and they shifted with it, getting used to each other and moving their bodies in time with the music, mirroring each other.

She realized she was actually having a pretty good time as they moved to the different beat, swaying and waving to the music.

It changed again into a slower song, and Carna didn't even think about it. When Miller held his hand out, she took it, putting her other hand on his shoulder, and they continued to move together, slower, though, and closer.

She wasn't sure quite what made the crowd clap as Miller twirled her, then pulled her close again.

"I think they're just happy to see that you're still able to move," he murmured, pulling her tight, with his hand on her lower back, hers on his shoulder, and their other two hands clasped between them.

She was close enough that when she moved her head, her temple brushed his cheek, feeling the stubble there.

"I'm kinda happy about that myself," she said, smiling and laughing just a little, maybe to hide the odd beating of her heart. She felt strangely out of breath. Although they were dancing, she hadn't been moving that much, not enough to wind herself.

But the feeling of being in Miller's arms, of having his face so close to hers, her hand in his, his arm around her, felt exactly right and perfectly natural, like stepping into his arms was like stepping into home.

She laid her head down on his shoulder, with her nose touching his neck.

She felt his head hover over hers as the music flowed around them.

They weren't really putting on a show. She almost forgot about the audience.

"I kinda forgot we were supposed to be entertaining people."

"I think you earned a little rest. And... I like this."

The last admission seemed a little hard-fought, and it made her throat tight.

"I do too," she said, softly because she couldn't get her throat to work any better.

It was crazy, but it was the first competition where she was actually bitterly disappointed when the buzzer sounded and it was over.

She didn't want to step back, didn't want to let go of him. Didn't want to feel his arm drop from hers, to have her hand slide out of his.

But the lights came back on—she hadn't even noticed when they'd dimmed—and the announcer came back over the megaphone.

"We'll find out our scores later, because the crowd is the judge of this contest!"

He said a few more things, talking about a few of the things that happened, but Carna didn't pay attention. She lifted her head. Miller seemed to be having the same problem she was. He didn't want to move.

"Are you sore?" she asked, not even thinking that maybe she should have offered her pain meds to him.

"No. Just...content."

She wasn't sure exactly what that meant, especially combined with his earlier statement, and she didn't want to probe into it too deeply. So she didn't.

Neither one of them moved until the announcer said it was time to walk to the pigpen.

"But I thought we were doing the Kiss Your Partner contest last?" Carna said as she reluctantly pulled away and gave a confused glance at the announcer and then back at Miller.

"I thought that's what the sheet said too."

She couldn't tell whether he had been looking forward to that as she had.

Of course, it made her a little nervous too, and she wasn't exactly sure why it had seemed to be the highlight of the contest to her, but she hadn't questioned herself over it, just knew it was something she wanted to do.

But...pigpen?

They walked out behind the stage, with many in the crowd heading out the doors as well.

Apparently, this contest had been a favorite of a lot of people, if the crowded area around the pigpens were any indication.

There were five makeshift pens and a one-hundred-pound hog in each pen.

"All right, contestants, when the bell rings, you will go into the pen, and both of you are to kiss your partner. The partner is the pig! Once both of you have caught and kissed it, ring the bell at the bottom of the gate and let us know you're done. You will be judged on time and style."

The announcer went on to introduce the contestants and say a little something about them.

Carna noticed that most of the crowd were lined up next to the pen that Miller and she had been assigned.

"You guys might be at the end, but you're the most entertaining!" one lady shouted as her husband stood with his arm around her, smiling benevolently and nodding.

Carna nodded her head, acknowledging the comment, and then looked up at Miller. "This is not what I thought this contest was going to be."

"Can I say I'm disappointed?" His tone held a bit of humor, but his eyes were dead serious.

She stared at him for just a moment before she breathed, "Me too."

It wasn't long before the announcer said, "If you're ready, let's go!"

Carna hurried to the gate and opened it, stepping into the pen and waiting for Miller to follow her.

They carefully latched the gate and then looked at their pig.

The pig had obviously been through this before and eyed them with not a little trepidation.

"I think they greased it," Miller said.

"It's shiny. I agree. And… I think they watered down the pen, because all of this mud is not natural."

"I'm so glad you said mud. I was thinking it was something else."

She looked down and studied the ground a little closer. "I think your first assessment was accurate, and I stand corrected."

"You're standing in the manure."

"That was helpful." She took a deep breath in, breathed out, held her fingers in a Zen position, and said, "White, sandy beaches."

"Could you do that after we catch the pig? I mean, I know we're going to lose the contest and everything, but we need to do what we're supposed to do."

"Right. Catch the pig. What's the strategy?" she asked, looking over at him like he had it all figured out.

He looked at the pig, looked back at her, and then said, "The strategy is to catch the pig."

She put her fingers together in a Zen position and began again, "White, sandy beaches."

"Carna. Later. You can do that the whole ride home."

"I'm gonna take a shower before we ride home."

"If you catch the pig, you can take a shower."

They advanced on the pig, putting a little bit of distance between them, both of them naturally trying to angle it toward a corner where they would have the best shot of using the fence to help them with their trapping endeavors.

It took three tries, and Carna was again covered from head to foot in mud, before Miller got a hand on the pig.

She couldn't help but laugh, since it was the first time that he had been dirty along with her.

"It's so nice to have company when I'm on the ground," she said, grinning at him.

"I'm glad I could make you happy. I was worried about that yesterday, but somehow today it doesn't seem quite as important."

"That's okay. You had a leg that time, we're going to get two next time."

Her fortune-telling ability turned out to be quite accurate in that instance any-way, since they cornered the pig, and she jumped on him. He wiggled out from underneath her, but that time Miller was able to get two hands on him, one on each back foot, and the pig squealed but was well and truly caught.

"It's a little heavy," Miller said as the pig struggled to get away. "You want me to hold it so you can kiss it first?"

Miller slowly stood, his hands down so that the pig's front feet were still on the ground, but his back feet were in the air.

Carna wasn't going to sit in the mud by herself, so she stood as well.

"Well?" she said, looking at the pig and then at Miller like he would have a plan.

Miller looked out at the crowd. They were cheering and chanting, "Kiss! Kiss! Kiss!"

"You know what, I don't want to kiss the pig." He let it go. "I'm kissing my real partner."

Carna's eyes got big while the pig scurried away.

He stepped toward her, and she had a good mind to back up, except she didn't want to.

She actually took a step forward. "I'm thinking you're talking about me."

"Sure am." He grinned at her, his eyes sparkling.

She figured that her eyes were probably sparkling as well. "I think this is a much better idea. It's what I wanted to begin with."

"Me too." By that time, he had an arm around her waist and another around her shoulders. "Maybe I should wait until I'm clean."

"I think I'm fine with you just the way you are."

"I'm good with you too. In fact, I'm a lot better than good. I... I've admired you every time you fell down and got back up. It's...hard not to fall in love with someone like that."

"What are you trying to say?" she asked, her brows raised as she lifted her gaze to him.

His eyes were dark and hooded, and there was no doubt he meant what he said.

She couldn't stop the short thrill that went through her as he said, "Someone said this trip could be life-changing. I didn't believe them. But I believe now they were absolutely correct. I love you."

Her eyes widened. That wasn't exactly what she thought he was going to say, but she knew immediately that she could return the sentiment. "I love you, too."

He grinned. "Even if I come in last?"

"Especially if you come in last. As long as it's with me."

"We're together. For sure."

He lowered his head and touched her lips with his, and even the cheering of the crowd couldn't make her want to back up or do anything but press closer as she put her arms around him and kissed him back.

Epilogue

"**I** didn't even make it to the barrel before I fell off." Carna grinned as the couples around her groaned. Abrielle glanced down at Miller's hand. The knuckles whitened, like he was agitated, but he still held Carna's hand carefully, like he was holding a precious treasure. Abrielle smiled.

"But that horse was one of the best, because it stopped." Miller touched his finger to the back of Carna's hand as he spoke, like he was assuring himself that it was still there.

"It sure did. So I didn't have to chase it around the arena trying to catch it. Although I did have to take it over to the fence to get back on. It was the tallest horse I rode."

"Hurts more to fall off a tall horse," Gideon, Piper's husband, observed. Their kids ran around the yard while the adults stood in a circle, chatting with the couple who had just returned home. They'd known they were coming and had gathered near the front porch of the big house to hear all about the competition.

The conversation flowed around, but Abrielle wasn't really listening. Instead she moved her head and lifted her brows at her husband, tilting her head just slightly toward Carna and Miller, just in case he missed their clasped hands.

His brows furrowed in confusion. Typical man. He hadn't noticed. Internally she shook her head in bemusement. What in the world did men notice since it seemed like they never saw anything obvious.

She waited, the group laughing and someone asking the newly returned couple another question before Smith finally saw the joined hands. His brows went way up as his eyes opened wide. Thankfully, Carna and Miller were knee-deep in another story and didn't notice the obviously shocked expression on Smith's face.

Abrielle felt a tightening around her middle and she froze for just a moment until it passed. She wanted to tell Smith not to draw attention to their hands because it would embarrass Carna, but she waited a second too long.

"Looks like you two got sidetracked from the competition and were more focused on each other. Maybe that's why you didn't win."

She needn't have worried, Carna just grinned and said, "We didn't win because I can't stay on a horse. Although maybe we didn't come in dead last. I think we might have pulled ourselves out of the pit with that last kissing move."

"We could demonstrate if you all think you'll ever be in a competition and need to win," Miller offered. The group groaned.

Eliza said, "Wait. You don't even know where you placed?"

Carna and Miller both looked a little abashed. "Well..." Miller swallowed. "I guess we got a little sidetracked with practicing the kissing - just in case we're ever in another contest, of course," he added to Carna's vigorous head-nodding. "And I supposed we weren't really thinking about placements when we found a quieter spot to -"

"That's okay." Smith held up his hand. "We don't need to know what you all were doing in your quiet spot."

Sighs of relief sounded around the loose circle.

"In case anyone is wondering, in the last three days, we've booked over fifty tours," Darby said, looking up from her phone where she had pulled up their booking app.

They group gasped and some of them clapped.

"Some of them are just half-day trips, but we have a few ten-day bookings." Darby's eyes glowed.

Abrielle smiled as the group celebrated, knowing the load her husband carried that no one else saw would be lightened considerably with that news, which made her smile. Indeed, his arm came around her and he pulled her closer to his side.

"How about that? Not only did your plan get them together, but it might have saved the ranch, too."

"It wouldn't have happened if you hadn't put them together," she whispered back, lifting her head so her words floated close to his ear.

"I think the lady is saying we make a pretty good team." Smith's lips brushed the side of her temple and his hand moved up her back.

"I can't disagree with that."

Abrielle sighed with contentment in her soul. Love for her husband, their ranch and their friends who were more like family to her, swelling deep in her heart. She didn't think it was possible to be happier.

"Hey, who's coming down the drive?" Miller asked as he lifted his head. Apparently he'd kissed Carna in celebration. Or maybe they were practicing more.

"Oh. We forgot to tell you. Monday foaled this morning. That's Lark coming down the drive to check it out."

Miller's face lit up and he turned to Carna. "Want to go see it?"

He no sooner had the words out of his mouth before Carna started walking toward the barn, obviously knowing how much it meant to him.

Abrielle smiled. They got each other and they were going to be so good together. She tried not to feel smug as

Lark's SUV stopped on the drive near where they all stood.

"Beautiful day," Lark said in greeting.

"Sure is." Smith turned toward her, his arm going around Abrielle as the others greeted Lark.

Somehow, despite the hardships of her past, which included a huge heartbreak, according to gossip in Sweet Water, Lark was always smiling and happy.

As Smith chatted with her for a few minutes, Abrielle tapped her chin, listening, but thinking, too. Someone needed to find a partner for Lark. A man of integrity and character, with a sense of humor and a deep loyalty. Someone who would make her laugh and cherish her like she deserved.

Not the man who broke her heart. Abrielle would like to shoot him herself. Except...maybe the man was just as heartsick as Lark and had reasons for what he had done. It was Abrielle's experience - hard fought - that sometimes motives weren't obvious and that when a person jumped to conclusions, she was usually wrong. That could be true in Lark's case.

Abrielle would give almost anything to know that story. Maybe someday.

In the meantime, maybe she'd send Billy on over to Lark's farm. Seemed like he had some work to do for their friendly veterinarian.

Enjoy this preview of Just a Cowboy's Happy Ever After, just for you!

Just a Cowboy's Happy Ever After

Chapter 1

"Go ahead and use the basement door. You can take it right to the kitchen and set it on the counter. That insulated wrap should keep it warm."

Lark Stryker directed Heavenne, one of the girls who lived with her, toward the church basement to keep her out of the way of the funeral goers, who were mostly going in the front door, the one leading directly to the sanctuary.

"Should I follow her?" Katrina asked, looking to Lark for guidance.

Heavenne and Katrina were both fifteen and had both been sent to Lark's care by their parents. Neither of them were terribly bad girls, they just needed someone to take an interest in them and give them a little bit of direction and attention.

Possibly disconnecting them from social media had been something else they'd needed.

"Yes. Yours should be able to go on the counter as well, but make sure you put it where the cold dishes are located."

If it weren't for the girls in her care, four of them right now—aside from Heavenne and Katrina, she had Kay and Erin, who were both thirteen—she wouldn't be here.

Taking a breath, she directed Kay to take the cake that she had made and follow the other two.

"Do you think anybody's going to like this?" Erin asked, biting her lip as she held the casserole she'd made.

It was the first time she'd made any-thing to take outside their home, which was a huge accomplishment for her, since when she first came to Lark's house, she didn't know how to cook at all.

"I think they're going to love it. That pierogi casserole is popular everywhere. And you did a great job on it," Lark said, putting a hand on Erin's shoulder and giving her a side hug.

Erin laid her head on Lark's arm just for a moment before she straightened. She was at that age where she was still so much a little girl but starting to become a woman as well.

Snuggling into another adult, one who was acting as a mother figure, wasn't exactly a mature thing for her to do.

Still, as long as she would allow hugs and other displays of affection, Lark would hand them out. Her mom had been excellent at that. Lark had never wondered whether her mom loved her. She said so, but she also showed them. Not just with hugs and the way she stroked Lark's hair or kissed her forehead, but because of the service that she did. Her mom would do anything to help her children, and Lark had that full confidence riding behind her all of her life.

There was no doubt in her mind that her mom thought she was amazing and she loved her.

Until she had gotten a little older, she was thirty-five now, she hadn't realized how valuable a feeling like that was. And the girls who came to her house typically didn't have that. Not about their mom and, more often, not about their dad either.

Most of the time, they weren't sure whether either one of their parents cared for them at all. They felt unwanted, like they were a mistake, in the way, an annoyance.

Sometimes they went out of their way to be those things, just because they didn't know how to be anything else. Or because the idea of having love and affection was too unusual and scary.

Sometimes dealing with girls like that was exhausting, but Lark relished it, along with her work as a veterinarian.

It kept her mind off other things.

Like Jeb Goodman. The man who was burying his wife today.

Steeling herself, pushing her shoulders back just a little, and grabbing the crock-pot with the sliced ham in it, she balanced it on her hip while she hit the button to shut the back of her car.

If it were just her, she wouldn't be here, but the girls who lived with her needed to see her serving and needed to learn to serve the community. Part of that was helping to provide food for the funerals that were held at the Sweet Water church.

Lark would have liked to back out of this one. Just because she'd managed to avoid Jeb ever since she'd graduated from vet school and started her own practice.

He never called her, despite owning a large dairy, and that was just fine by her.

Once upon a time, she thought she would marry him.

He refused. She might have fallen into a deep depression, but someone, she wasn't sure who, had offered to pay for vet school.

She corresponded with her benefactor all through college and vet school, continuing even after she graduated. Which was another part of why she was at the funeral today—her benefactor, after years of refusing her offers to meet so she could thank him in person, finally asked to meet her. She'd agreed immediately, of course, and they'd set up a time that happened to be after the funeral and meal, meeting at the big oak tree behind the old white church in Sweet Water.

She couldn't think of that meeting without being a little nervous. The man, whoever he was, had paid for all her schooling, had bought her farm, and had provided a way for her to help the girls who lived with her.

Having the girls was her way of giving back to the community, since her bene-factor had invested so heavily into her.

If it hadn't been for him, his encour-aging letters, his monetary support, she wasn't sure where she would be today.

Regardless, for the immediate future, she figured it was probably too much for her to hope to make it through the rest of the day without seeing Jeb, so she steeled herself and tried to remind herself that she was a mature, grown woman, and she could handle seeing an old crush. Even one who had so brutally rejected her.

And then married someone else.

"Lark! Sweetheart. Let me help you with that." Her mother hurried toward Lark.

"Mom, I've got it. You can get the door though," Lark said with a smile at her mom who, despite her advancing years, still walked with a spring in her step, even if it had gotten a little slower over the years.

"Where's your husband?" she asked about the man her mom had married several years ago. It was about time too, since Lark's dad had died when she was just a little girl. Her mom had raised all ten of her children on her own.

"He carried my stuff in, and I just came back out to the car for these." Her mom held up napkins.

That didn't really make Lark feel bad, even though the thought crossed her mind that if she had a husband, he would be carrying the crockpot for her most likely. Although, she knew there were women who were married to men who didn't think to do anything kind for their wives.

"I know a funeral isn't a great place to meet people, but there's someone I want you to meet."

"Mom." Lark leaned her head to the side and gave her mom a look that she hadn't used in a really long time.

It used to be when she was in college, and especially vet school, her mom would ask almost every other weekend whether she had found someone.

She never told her mom that she was still pining over Jeb. It seemed like when she gave her heart, she gave it completely and couldn't take it back, even if it was thrown at her. Or maybe she accidentally ducked when he threw it, and it missed her, landing somewhere where she couldn't find it.

She almost laughed at the whimsical idea. She just...wasn't someone who fell in love easily, she supposed.

"I know. I learned a long time ago that it's just best for me to keep my mouth shut and to stay out of my children's business. But this is a special case. Please believe me when I say that I have your best interest at heart."

"I know you do, Mom. You always have. I appreciate it."

She'd let her mom introduce her to whoever she wanted to, just because her mom had earned that right, over and over and over again. She couldn't imagine having a better mother.

But she wasn't the slightest bit interested in meeting someone. Not now, not ever. She'd put everything on the line when she'd fallen for Jeb, and she supposed there were some things a person just couldn't recover from.

"All right. You take these things in, set them on the counter, and you come on back out here."

"Mom, it's a funeral."

"I know. I know. But I'm telling you, this is the chance of a lifetime. And I know that that's a pretty big statement, but just listen, it's like this: my husband worked with his dad. They grew up together. His dad decided to not exactly go off-grid, but to be a little more self-sufficient, just raise his kids and his family on a farm. They ended up having six boys and six girls."

"Twelve kids?" It was unusual to find anyone with ten children in their family, the way she had with her siblings. It just wasn't done anymore. Unless a person was Amish or Mennonite.

"Yes. Twelve kids. They actually have more than we do."

"That's rare."

"I told you." Her mom smiled, and it wasn't hard to hear the barely contained excitement in her voice. "So, you have that in common with him. And the entire family has just relocated to a ranch just outside of Sweet Water. We have the Sweet Water Ranch, of course. And we have Sweet Briar Ranch, plus we have the Coleman trucking company and the Baldwin sale barn. Now, we have the Sweet View ranch, and all twelve siblings are going to be living on it."

"All twelve?"

"Apparently the parents were killed in a car accident. It happened right by the ranch that they were living on down in Wyoming, and the siblings decided they wanted a fresh start."

Lark's mom went on about the man she wanted Lark to meet. Lark couldn't disagree that he sounded like a really nice guy. Successful. A family man. Someone who was loyal to his siblings, even when he might be better off leaving and doing something on his own.

Those were all things she admired in someone. But since she'd been fifteen, there had only been one man for her and she hadn't really been able to look at anyone else.

She didn't think, despite the twenty years that had gone by, that anything had changed.

"Oh! There he is!" her mom said, grabbing her arm and practically dragging her along.

It was so out of character for her mom. Normally, she just sat back and allowed things to happen. She prayed a lot but didn't do a lot of manipulation in her children's lives.

Because it was so unusual, Lark felt like she had to go along with it. Her mom asked for so very little, after giving her so very much.

"Ezra!" her mom called, making Lark feel like she was twelve and giving her the strongest desire to bury her head in the sand. "Ezra! This is my daughter who I was telling you about!"

"Mom. I'll follow you. You don't have to drag me like I'm a sled," Lark gritted out between teeth that were clamped together.

Her mom slowed, looking at where she held tight to Lark's arm. She loosened her fingers and said softly, "I'm sorry. I just...just want you to be happy." Her mom turned and gave Lark the most tender look. It made Lark feel guilty for even saying anything.

"Mom. I am happy."

"But you need to be married. You need a mate. A partner. Someone who's going to support you and be with you, who will love you the way you deserve to be loved."

"Mom. I don't need that. I have Jesus."

Her mom's mouth opened, then closed, then opened again. Finally, she closed it, pressed her lips together, and shook her head. "How can I argue with that?"

"You're the one who taught it to me. Of course God wants us to get married. He didn't create us to be alone, but He also wanted us to be able to depend on Jesus and say that He is enough."

"I know."

"Did you call me?" a man's voice said, causing both Lark and her mother to turn.

It was a voice that spoke of responsibility and hard work and loyalty and character.

Lark couldn't fault her mom. If she were looking for a man, this man would be an excellent choice. How he managed to make it to be her age and unmarried was anyone's guess.

Maybe he was divorced, but he didn't look like the kind of man who would leave his wife, and a woman would have to be crazy to walk away from a man with character like that.

But sometimes people made huge mistakes and never recovered from them.

"I called you. I want you to meet my daughter, Lark. She's the veterinarian around Sweet Water."

"Along with my partner," Lark added, because she couldn't take all the credit.

"Lark. I've heard a lot about you. It's good to meet you," the man said, holding out his hand. "I'm Ezra."

The man's handshake was firm, his hand dry and rough with calluses.

He would be a good man to have as a friend and definitely a great asset to the community, but Lark couldn't say that she was the slightest bit interested in being anything more than friends with him.

She supposed young love died hard for most people, but for her, it seemed to be like a bad weed that just wouldn't die.

"It's good to meet you. I'm Lark. I heard you're moving in with your entire family."

"Yeah. We needed a change. We're relocating, all of us together. I know it's a little bit weird, but anyone with twelve kids in their family these days is going to be a little weird."

Lark laughed and agreed with that assessment.

They chatted for a bit, with Lark trying to put the effort in that her mom expected of her.

She might be thirty-five, but she still wanted to please her mom. She didn't figure that would ever change.

Still, as the parking lot got more crowded, she finally said, "I better go. My girls are helping with the meal, and I need to make sure that everything's happening the way it should. Are you still good to take them home?" she asked her mom. She'd agreed to take the girls so

Lark could go to her meeting at the old church.

Her mom nodded, but Lark could see the disappointment in her mother's face, and it cut at her heart.

She didn't want to disappoint her mom. Actually, she knew that her mom was pleased with whatever she did. The problem was, she worried about Lark.

Lark couldn't blame her. Any of the girls that had been in her care, no matter for how short of a time, she wanted them to succeed in life, to be happy.

That's all her mom wanted for her, and Lark couldn't fault her.

The problem was, there would never be anyone for her but Jeb.

Lark went into the kitchen, chatting with the ladies who were there and praising her girls for the good job that they had been doing.

The funeral was about to start, and while Lark wished she could stay in the basement, she herded her girls together, and they went up the stairs. The girls saw some other teens sitting in the middle of the rows of pews, and Lark nodded when they asked if they could sit in the pew directly behind them, which was half-empty.

They walked away, and Lark stopped for just a moment, taking a breath and looking at the man she hadn't seen for years.

He stood at the front of the church, his profile to her, facing the head of the coffin. It was still open.

She supposed they'd shut it before the funeral began, but for now, people milled about, standing at the coffin, talking to the man in low voices, although he didn't have much to say.

Jeb never really did talk much. She could tell within the first thirty seconds that hadn't changed at all.

It made her smile. She talked enough for both of them. At least she had when she was younger. She supposed she didn't talk quite as much now as she did then.

Still, she always thought that was a good balance in their personalities. He didn't talk, she did. He wasn't very so-cial, she was. He was very serious, she couldn't help but be happy and smiling about pretty much everything.

There were a lot of opposites in their personalities, but their core values were exactly the same.

She swallowed. Jeb saw things differ-ently about their relationship, though. It was one of the few things that they disagreed on.

Of course, she didn't know they dis-agreed on it until she proposed to him.

His wife lay in front of him. Lark could see the thatch of silver hair, the hands folded over the chest, lying still above the blanket tucked around the body.

Her heart cramped, seizing and feeling like it stopped in her chest before it started beating hard and slow, big, painful thumps.

It was hard to pull breath into her lungs, but she straightened her back to provide more room, until she could feel her lungs fill and blow out slowly against the pain.

She could do this. She could walk up the aisle, sit down, and attend this funeral. Even while Jeb sat just feet away from her.

She could go back downstairs and serve the meal, chatting and smiling at people, being kind, even if that included serving Jeb.

Somehow, she doubted he'd come through the line.

Still, if he did, she could handle it.

What she wasn't sure she could handle was having Jeb be single and living not very far from her at all.

Even though he'd rejected her, clearly and deliberately, she still could see herself driving to his house, begging him to take her. She'd probably have nightmares about doing that very thing.

She wanted to have more class than that. More pride. Except, God resisted the proud but gave grace to the humble. He gave the humble their wishes while taking from the proud.

God, I've been nothing but humble when it came to Jeb.

Still, it wouldn't be any good now anyway. What if he did accept her? They didn't even know each other. And she didn't have time to do what she'd done before. And he wouldn't.

Walking slowly forward, her dress swishing around her ankles, she went to the pew where the girls had made room for her at the end, and sat down, her back straight, her eyes forward. She would make it through. She always made it through.

Pick up your copy of Just a Cowboy's Happy Ever After by Jessie Gussman today!

A Gift from Jessie

View this code through your smart phone camera to be taken to a page where you can download a FREE ebook when you sign up to get updates from Jessie Gussman! Find out why people say, "Jessie's is the only newsletter I open and read" and "You make my day brighter. Love, love, love reading your newsletters. I don't know where you find time to write books. You are so busy living life. A true blessing." and "I know from now on that I can't be drinking my morning coffee while reading your newsletter – I laughed so hard I sprayed it out all over the table!"

Claim your free
book from Jessie!

Escape to more faith-filled romance series by Jessie Gussman!

The Complete Sweet Water, North Dakota Reading Order:

Series One: Sweet Water Ranch Western Cowboy Romance (11 book series)

Series Two: Coming Home to North Dakota (12 book series)

Series Three: Flyboys of Sweet Briar Ranch in North Dakota (13 book series)

Series Four: Sweet View Ranch Western Cowboy Romance (10 book series)

Spinoffs and More! Additional Series You'll Love:

<u>Jessie's First Series: Sweet Haven Farm (4 book series)</u>

<u>Small-Town Romance: The Baxter Boys (5 book series)</u>

<u>Bad-Boy Sweet Romance: Richmond Rebels Sweet Romance (3 book series)</u>

<u>Sweet Water Spinoff: Cowboy Crossing (9 book series)</u>

<u>Holiday Romance: Cowboy Mountain Christmas (6 book series)</u>

<u>Small Town Romantic Comedy: Good Grief, Idaho (5 book series)</u>

<u>True Stories from Jessie's Farm: Stories from Jessie Gussman's Newsletter (3 book series)</u>

<u>Reader-Favorite! Sweet Beach Romance: Blueberry Beach (8 book series)</u>

<u>Cowboy Mountain Christmas Spinoff: A Heartland Cowboy Christmas (9 book series)</u>

<u>Blueberry Beach Spinoff: Strawberry Sands (10 book series)</u>